the Gospel according to Dara

THE GOSPEL ACCORDING TO DARA

the Gospel according to Dara

BILL GOLEMBESKI

two
peas
publishing

COLUMBIA, TENNESSEE

Tomorrow's up for sale again I heard the prophet say.
—Chris Simpson of Magna Carta

FOR MOM

rather Suggestive Photos

OTIS NEEDED A HAIRCUT. That's what I said as I looked into his Hushpuppy eyes. I said, "Otis, you really need a haircut." That's what I said.

Otis was a basset hound.

He looked, for the most part, like every other basset in God's prototypical plan. His legs were short, really short. His body was low, long, and lumpy. Perhaps he really did need a haircut. That was odd. Otis looked like all other basset hounds except for one thing: He had several hairs that sprouted like a sprig of goatsbeard from the top of his basset head. Those hairs looked like a two-fingered peace sign from some aged hippy thumbing a ride along some aged hippy highway. They looked like two trees grafted into the closeness of an embrace. They looked like two trees I had come to cherish.

The tips of those hairs were white—like they had been dipped in Tom Sawyer's whitewash. No comb could ever control those hairs. No brush could make those hairs stay in place. They were outlaws of the follicle world. So we all accepted the fact that Otis suffered from a bad case of terminal cowlick. That's just the way it was. There was very little any one of us could do except threaten him with the barber's shears, but that would be

RATHER SUGGESTIVE PHOTOS

like plugging Old Faithful's geyser spray. So those hairs were the joke of our neighborhood — a joke providing a punch line for sad and, perhaps. profound words, words we never managed to say to the very people we loved.

"Otis," I said again, "you really do need a haircut."

He glanced at me with his sagging jowls and panted several times quickly. He looked like he was laughing. Dogs often appear to be laughing. Maybe that's why I like them so much.

There was one more thing that made old Otis so different from all other basset hounds. He spent most of his saggy time lounging by the side of our neighborhood road. He watched everybody and every car. I truly believe he watched every leaf fall from every tree. He watched every bike and every squirrel that scurried across his street.

Otis watched us, and we watched him as he watched us live our lives.

Otis belonged to Mrs. Fletcher, an elderly woman who lived in a small house that stood on three acres of sacred soil. All the other houses on our block were a part of our picturesque suburbia. We lived in square houses on square lots, and all the houses had the same mailbox. Every garage was attached to its house. That was important. For the most part, we all received the same mail with advertisements, and we wanted the same Christmas and birthday cards.

Mrs. Fletcher had been our music teacher — although I can't recall paying her any money. Her three acres of sacred soil had never been developed into square lots. Her sacred soil was the birthplace of many beautiful oak trees that grew tall and thick on her property. Her three acres had never left Eden — an Eden lost to commercial development everywhere else. This bit of green space, smack dab in the middle of suburbia, made an Adam and

THE GOSPEL ACCORDING TO DARA

Eve of us all, although I doubt seriously the original Adam and Eve ever bothered with junk mail or Christmas cards.

There were many trees, but Mrs. Fletcher had pampered two old oaks with tender care. We called them Noah and Eloise. They were named after her grandparents. Mrs. Fletcher once told me they had planted these oaks on their first wedding anniversary, which they had celebrated in 1878. She lifted one of the vines of ivy that spiraled up Eloise's old trunk.

"This ivy," she said, "is older than I am. That's really too old." She paused and rubbed the green leaf. "This dies and then comes back every year. And it's taller. It's taller every year."

I noticed her hands were bent with arthritis. She could no longer use them to play the piano.

"Is it the same ivy?" I asked.

"Nothing really ever changes," she told me. "It dies. But it doesn't change."

Then she gently placed the ivy back on the broad circumference of Eloise. Her hands were crooked, and I was glad I was able to play all the music she had given to me. I wanted to play that music because her hands were so old and so twisted.

One time, she showed me a marked indentation on each tree. The sunken notches were just random scars as far as I could see. Tree bark is tree bark. The tree had simply grown a lumpy circle around a spot.

I remember Mrs. Fletcher tracing Noah's name with her old finger pressed patiently against the bark.

"Ellie carved his name here," she said. "You probably don't care, but you should look. Then you'll care. Just look. Imagine those letters. Imagine Noah's name." Then she said again, "Nothing ever changes. We just lose the ability to see it."

I wanted to see what was not there. It was a mystery. It was

RATHER SUGGESTIVE PHOTOS

like the Loch Ness Monster or the Shroud of Turin. It was a mystery like Santa Claus or the wandering dead on a foggy All Hallows' Eve.

I had given up on mystery at the time. And I truly believed old Mrs. Fletcher was wrong. Some things do change. Mystery — the belief in things unseen — was buried in a local cemetery, a tombstone marked with two deaths. That's why I just couldn't see those letters — Noah's name — etched into the heart of that old oak tree. Life is life, and death is death.

That's what I thought.

I remember her finger as it slowly moved over the scarred tree bark.

"You should care. You really should care. Because Ellie carved his name here. Do you see his name? It says Noah." She paused and pointed to the other tree. "And Noah carved Ellie's name over there." She reached and touched the other oak tree. She gently rubbed a rough and uneven spot. "Do you see her name? It says Eloise. It's right here. Do you see it? He carved her name right here."

I wanted to see Eloise's name. I really did. But a gravestone is a gravestone.

I desperately wanted to see her name like every decent person wants to see the truth, just like we all want Jesus to rise on Easter Sunday and the Green Bay Packers to win every week. I honestly didn't see anything but the scars on the bark of an old oak tree that simply wanted to heal itself as best it could.

I'd do the same thing if I were that tree.

"Sure," I lied. "I think I see a few of the letters of her name."

Mrs. Fletcher smiled and said, "You're a good boy. You're a sad boy. You're lying to an old woman to make her feel better. You will see." Again, she carefully rubbed her old fingers over the bark. "You'll see. Just like I see. Things don't change. Every year the names are covered. Each tree tries to heal itself, but they are there. The names are there. Eloise and Noah. You'll see. Their names are still there.

"Someday these trees will grow too old and just fall over. The wind will blow these trees over, or they will get cut down. Then you will see. Those names will still be etched in the bark, notched into the very heart with all the age rings of growth. You'll see. Their names will still be there. Eloise and Noah will still be there. They will dance again."

Well, the actual story of Noah and Eloise is a history best left for another time. Suffice it to say the space between the two oaks was the favorite lounging area for Otis. He liked the narrow space, and that narrow space liked him. He propped himself up with his short front legs, while his chubby low-rider of a basset body rested like an unbaked loaf of thick French bread. His tail had a white tip, and it wagged a little bit whenever a car slowed and the passing driver within honked a horn at him.

Everybody in the neighborhood knew Otis. We called him the Roadside Basset. We all yelled, "Hey, Roadside!" as we passed those old oaks. We knew Otis was always there. Of course he was there. He was the Roadside Basset who filled that meager space—the meager space between all our lives. Otis gave community to neighbors who probably didn't even like each other all that much, if the truth be told. That silly old basset gave us an identity. He was our flag, and a flag is always grown from the very soil that it celebrates.

We loved those old oaks, and we really loved that old basset. Otis, with his sagging face and sad eyes, was the focal point of our neighborhood. We honked, and we waved. Expressing emotions is easy when tickling a dog or saluting a flag. We loved

RATHER SUGGESTIVE PHOTOS

those two old oaks, and we loved that old Roadside Basset. That basset face presented the irony of life, and we humans need to find that irony. That's why we loved that old dog.

Much later in life, I saw that same irony again.

George W. Bush was president, and I was in some nameless hotel in Winnipeg, Canada. The hotel didn't have air-conditioning, so I sweated with mid-July perspiration. Dogs and people panted everywhere. I met an ex-patriot truck-driver American in the hotel parking lot. He owned a one-eyed dog. I noticed the missing eye. Then this truck driver told me everyone saw that missing eye, but he saw the one good eye.

Bless the wind that carries this memory back to me. He and his dog were companions for life. I have loved Canada ever since that morning. He told me, while tenderly holding his dog, that his brother Kenny had been killed in Vietnam during the Tet Offensive. He waited for Kenny's body to be laid in the earth. He said he kissed the ground in which his brother rested. The guy held his one-eyed dog and said patience is a gift from God. He said he kissed the ground in which his brother rested, and then he left for Canada because he didn't want to wait for his own draft notice.

He just crossed the border.

That was that.

Canadian is Canadian. American is American. Everything else is everything else.

I asked him if he missed America. I just assumed missing is missing. The guy shook his head. His dog did the very same thing. He laughed and told me he often thought about driving to the border, standing on the precipice of North Dakota, and just taking a piss — a piss right on America.

Then he hugged his one-eyed dog.

I didn't know what to say. I loved America. I loved Wisconsin. I loved North Dakota. I had driven through the state on my trip to Winnipeg and had stopped to see a white buffalo — a sacred animal for the Lakota Sioux, who refused to charge a fee to see their buffalo. I didn't agree with the truck driver's urge to urinate. But then, I hadn't knelt to kiss the grave of my dead brother. I had never worried about a draft notice. I didn't live in Canada.

The guy laughed again and mentioned the cable news. All hotels in 2008 had cable television. The Miss Universe Pageant had been held in, of all places, Vietnam. "Can you believe that?" he asked.

I nodded.

"And your Jerry Springer guy was the host, him and some Spice Girl." He asked again, "Can you believe that Jerry Springer and Sugar Spice were in Vietnam?" I swear his dog chuckled.

"And your Miss USA fell flat on her ass." He continued to laugh. "Some things never change."

I couldn't argue with that. There was no need to argue; falling on your ass is falling on your ass, but I didn't have the heart or the guts to confess that the shirt I wore, as we spoke, had been made in Vietnam. So I just petted his dog and said something nice about his truck.

Sometimes, that's all there is to say.

Of course, I wasn't thinking of any of this as I sat next to old Otis while he rested between Noah and Eloise, patiently watching all the passing people and cars.

The year was 1980, and Ronald Reagan was about to be

elected president. Who would have imagined that years later as I listened to a Canadian truck driver say he wanted to urinate on North Dakota, I would be afraid to tell him that the shirt I wore was made in Vietnam? In 1980, we hated Russia because it was a communist country. It was the "evil empire" — the "dark star" wanting to destroy democracy.

Russia had funded the Viet Cong. We truly believed democracy was a good enough cause for which to die — until the itchy palms of corporate greed deduced that investment in totalitarian dictatorships was a much better gamble than chancing a bet on a fledgling ballot box of a government that was one bullet away from a coup.

A friend named Duffy Finch had been killed in Vietnam. He died for democracy.

His death had not changed one damn thing in the world.

So I thought about Ronald Reagan, Duffy, and Duffy's sister, Debbie. It was impossible to smile. All I knew was that we were in big trouble because old Otis was not at all interested in the process of procreation. That was too bad because we desperately needed an heir to his sagging basset genes. I was trying really hard to get Otis to take even a modicum of interest in various pictures of the photo spread in *Pup and Paw* magazine. I held the magazine in front of those sad old eyes.

"Look!" I said, as I showed him the centerfold. "This is Agnes. She's a champion basset. Isn't she cute?" I watched that old face as it glanced at the photo of Agnes, the champion basset — Agnes in full sprint. "Don't you think she's cute? Don't you think she's sexy?"

One old basset eyebrow raised itself for a moment. Then it resigned itself to disinterest. Otis sighed.

I sighed, too. Then I turned the page. "Come on, Otis," I

pleaded. "This one's really good-looking!" I tried to be enthusiastic. "Wouldn't you like to meet her? She's on her doggie bed. Look! I don't think she's even wearing a collar!

"And tomorrow," I said suddenly, "tomorrow is the Fourth of July! You know, independence and fireworks!" I tried to inject a sense of urgency into the situation. I held the glossy photo for Otis' inspection.

His eyes slowly moved back and forth.

"Her name is Oreo. You know, like the cookie. Wouldn't you like to meet her, Otis?"

He wagged his tail when he heard that word. He knew the word "cookie." He wanted a cookie. Apparently, Mrs. Fletcher had given him too many treats. He barked several times. He wanted food.

"No, no, no!" I shook my head. "No, Otis. Not that kind of cookie." I showed him the picture again. "This is Oreo! You should like these pictures. She's on her doggie bed. She doesn't have her collar on. We guys like this sort of thing.

"Come on, Otis," I pleaded. "This is important. This is really important!"

Was I sarcastic? I suppose so, really. I was showing dog pornography to this old basset who didn't seem to care about sex. How could I not be sarcastic? Unfortunately, Otis had shared too many desserts with Mrs. Fletcher not to remember how much he loved his sweets.

He barked several times. There was no sarcasm in those barks. I think he wanted a cookie.

"No," I spoke slowly. "Otis, I don't have dessert. Look at these pictures. Please. Look at these pictures. Aren't they sexy?"

Otis just looked sadly at the photo. Then he looked at me and sighed in a saggy way.

I sighed, too. I didn't yet know about all the irony in humor and love and whatever. I just knew we were in trouble, and it wasn't just because Otis needed a haircut. It wasn't because he didn't like the pictures in *Pup and Paw*.

We were in trouble because old Mrs. Fletcher, his owner and the beloved caretaker of Eloise and Noah, had died.

Hope of Rain

FOR SOME REASON, I WAS THINKING ABOUT Duffy
Finch. I played football with him. He threw me my first real
touchdown pass. We talked about all the girls in the neighborhood. He somehow had come into possession of a bottle of
brandy. That was a big deal.

He also had a *Playboy* magazine. That was a bigger deal.

Duffy was killed in Vietnam. He wasn't much older than I
was when he died. I didn't go to his funeral. God must know
why I didn't go, because I don't.

I knew his sister. Her name was Debbie Finch. In a strange
and hopelessly young way, I loved her. Debbie died long before
her brother was killed in what the nightly news called the Tet
Offensive.

I cried twice for that family. Even today, I cry for them.

It's the only way I am still able to pray.

"At least when you die," I said, "you don't have to sit through
anybody else's funeral."

"Joshua Toss!" Lydia said under her breath. Then she kicked

me. "Be decent. This is Mrs. Fletcher. This is her funeral."

"Don't kick me! You can't do that at a funeral. What would Mrs. Fletcher say?"

Lydia kicked me again.

"She'd say, 'Kick him again.'"

"In some cultures," I said with stupid authority, "if you kick somebody at a funeral, you have to shave your head ritualistically twice a week and walk backward for seven years, or until the spirit of the dead person returns and says you don't have to do that stuff anymore." Then I quickly moved out of striking distance.

Lydia Maenad had one enduring charm: She kicked at the world. She sang protest songs; she held protest signs; she yelled protest slogans; she shook her protest fist at a society that, in her opinion, earned that fiery fist in every heartbeat of its existence.

She knew the songs of Bob Dylan, Phil Ochs, Joan Baez, Pete Seeger, and all the others. In her mind, she had "overcome" years ago, and it was about time for everybody else to "overcome," "row the boat ashore," figure out what was "blowing in the wind," know about the "sounds of silence," sing "Kumbaya," proclaim the fact that "we're not marching anymore," and, well, know how to "imagine" a much better world than our current state of affairs. Lately, she had embraced punk rock, and, to tell the truth, I was extremely jealous.

Liddy dressed with a combination that did, indeed, spin any locker dial back and forth several times. She wore a short skirt with colored tights, and she always punctuated those tights with high-topped Converse tennis shoes. She was the Earth goddess ever so slightly morphed into Siouxsie Sue and every one of her punk rocker Banshees.

Did I say I was jealous? You bet I was.

THE GOSPEL ACCORDING TO DARA

I had given up on everything. I even dressed like I had given up, whatever that means. I wanted to yell and scream. I wanted to jump up and down and get damn mad for once in my life, but I always managed to defuse any emotion with some witty bit of sarcasm. I was always and everywhere prepared to be witty. It was like a curse, believe me, because it was always there. I always told a joke, and people always laughed. The curse was always the curse.

That's why I was so jealous of Lydia. She could get mad—but not me, I could never get mad. I just couldn't get angry. I was the punch line in a funny birthday card that nobody had to buy.

I always tell people that my third-grade report card said, in broad teacher scrawl, "Joshua Toss seems to be much too sincere for his age." I also tell everyone the teacher said, "Young Joshua draws birds very well."

Other kids solved complex math problems. Other kids understood the mating ritual of a mealworm. Other kids knew the capital of South Dakota.

I drew birds well and was too sincere. So that was that. It was the report card etched in the stone gates of hell.

Years later, still without an exact knowledge of the mealworm's mating ritual, I wrote a "drug song" that was added to my list of unforgettable achievements. Everybody seemed to know that song. Drawing birds well in third grade, being sincere, and writing a fake drug song are all equally dangerous things, I know. They are all carved on the toilet-stall walls in whatever hell anyone cares to inhabit. I suppose that's why I am stuck with the reality of my life. Perhaps there is no escape at all. I should be content to draw birds, to be sincere, and to write humorous songs. That should be enough for me, but it wasn't enough.

IN HOPE OF RAIN

I was envious of Lydia. She sang angry songs. She got damn mad. She could kick things.

Sometimes she kicked me.

I just laughed a lot.

Sincere? I know! Talking to a dog about sex with other dogs is a long way from Mr. Sensitive New-Aged Guy who loves Mannheim Steamroller's Christmas album. But things change, don't they? I once saw Debbie Finch's eyes. They were deep blue eyes. I vowed never to draw another bird.

One time, I met a woman—a recovering alcoholic. She wore a T-shirt that read "I Haven't Had a Drink in Three Days." I wanted to tell her I hadn't drawn a bird since Debbie Finch died. I wanted to tell her about Debbie's deep-blue eyes. Sincerity was erased from my soul like the cardinal, the robin, or the blue jay I never managed to draw. Sincerity was left in the hope my third-grade teacher inked into my report card.

So I said to Lydia, "I read somewhere that a woman kicked somebody else at a funeral and really offended the great spirit world, and that woman had to do all the other stuff, except she had to shave her head three times a week, walk backward really fast, and she could only sing songs by Captain and Tennille. So, if you keep kicking me, you'll have to sing 'Love Will Keep Us Together.'" I paused. "And then, when you die, you'll have to go to a place in hell where you'll have to star in your own variety show, perform stupid skits, and sing 'Muskrat Love' every week because the sponsors want all the people in hell to tune in and listen to you sing the Captain and Tennille songs and buy their products.

I knew that would hurt. Friends know how to hurt each other. I had known Lydia for so long. Of course, I had been in the audience at the city amateur show when she was twelve. I was always a year older and a year wiser than my Liddy. This was pre–short skirt, colored tights, and high-topped tennis shoe Lydia. This was the sweet-song-and-dance Lydia who, with her dance partner, Ollie Meadows, sang their way into third place with a rendition of the very same Captain and Tennille's ode to "Muskrat Love," which would, indeed, keep them together.

Second place, it should be noted, was awarded to Stevie Mays, who did his magic act, which included sawing his younger sister, Sarah, in half.

The big winners were several local malcontents who wore Kiss makeup and lip-synced their way into talent-show stardom with a rousing rendition of a Kiss song called "Rock and Roll All Night." The only thing authentic about their performance was the cherry bomb they blew off as they mimicked the rock-star parody of their rock 'n' roll heroes.

The crowd went wild.

That said, I must confess an undying fascination with Lydia's Toni Tennille impersonation on the talent-show stage so many years ago. She and Ollie Meadows, ever dapper as the Captain behind his keyboards, sang their youthful hearts out in front of an audience who, let's face it, preferred a lip-synced Kiss song and a second-rate magic act.

I watched Lydia with a mixture of love, jealousy, and a thousand other teenage emotions entangled within my mixed and muddled talent-show-spectator existence. I would like to think that, after so many years, I have sorted through those emotions, but I am never quite certain about that. I clapped after Lydia's performance. I clapped. Perhaps I clapped because I truly did care about her with the notes of some melody that far exceeded a talent-show performance of top-forty hit songs.

Lydia's eyes, as she stood in the funeral parlor, turned the color of the molten sea floor I had watched during countless films in science class. She understood my Captain and Tennille comment for what it was meant to be. It became so hot the undertaker had to turn the air-conditioning up a notch or two.

Belle laughed.

Let me tell you about our Belle. This, of course, was before she was shot and destined to spend so much time in a wheelchair. I truly do like to remember her as she laughed at my comment. We all stood some distance from Mrs. Fletcher in her coffin. I swear the old woman's lips smiled as Belle laughed. Belle made the birds I was once able to draw quite happy. Someone once said that the birds wouldn't sing in the morning until Belle was outside. I really doubt that. That made her sound like she was Mrs. St. Francis or something. She wasn't like that at all. Her laugh had a stainless-steel edge to its lilt. Belle's laugh could examine the proximity of pain while still pausing to retain a fraction of an inch of redemption. Her laugh made me laugh.

One time at some sort of folk festival, I watched as Celtic dancers performed with sabers crossed at their feet. I watched closely as each dancer inched closer to a blade's razor edge. I watched their eyes, and I watched their feet, as each glance and each toe dared all other glances and toes to place their fraction of an inch of hope closer to the blade.

THE GOSPEL ACCORDING TO DARA

Belle's laugh was just like that dance. It was a truth and a dare that lured everyone an inch closer to the razor's edge. It was a siren's call laughing in disbelief at its own seductive appeal. People say she charmed all the wildlife. In truth, she was no saint. People create myths in retrospect, and myths are often more real than the truth they cover. So, I will just add to the hyperbole and state here that, yes, Mrs. Fletcher did smile. Belle's laugh could make the dead happy.

Sometimes warm memories are all we have—warm memories of all that has passed before us. Perhaps that's why we like thrift stores so much. Real stores contain stuff to buy, new stuff without any history. There is no memory. The thrift stores contain warm memories that understand warm dust. Belle's laugh was a truth and a dare, but it was also hauntingly old—like a thrift store. Of course, this was all before she was shot. After that, she barely smiled at all. After that, dusty warm shelves were much more difficult to find.

So, a bit more about our Belle: I thought she was the complete opposite of her younger sister Lydia. I thought she never protested anything. I was wrong, terribly wrong. She was every bit the rebel her sister was. She just laughed a lot more, so we never quite figured her out.

Years later, I gazed into the darkness of Halloween night—a great night for dead souls. This is my favorite celebration of the year. I had given candy to spirits who looked like Batman, Spiderman, and my personal favorite superhero—Green Lantern. I gave them all candy.

They all said "Thanks."

Then a solitary girl in street clothes approached my door. She wasn't wearing a costume. I said, "Where's your costume?"

She laughed.

"Where's your costume?" I asked again.

"Trick or treat," she said.

I looked into her deep blue eyes. They were like the ocean currents that swept through the ghosts of the Titanic who still secretly wished for a seat in a lifeboat.

"Trick or treat," she said again. Then I realized her laugh was her costume. I knew my laugh was my costume, too.

She took a small Snickers Bar out of her bag and gave it to me.

I said, "Trick or treat." She gave me an odd look—a look through the eyes of a fish that had tried to read the expensive dinner menu of an ill-fated White Star liner every day for too many nights. She said, "You see, every time I get a piece of candy, I just want more. So I don't need any more." Her laughter was sweet salvation in the crisp, opulent air—a dense darkness penetrated softly by a melting candle: a candle that illuminated a grinning pumpkin face staring at the door of our American dream of a house complete with a three-stall garage.

I still believed Mrs. Fletcher smiled. But she was dead. Perhaps it was just the thought of her gracefully caressing those trees.

Home movies of her played in my head. She had taught all of us music. Lydia learnt her first protest songs from her. Mrs. Fletcher was one of the few adults I have ever known who, quite simply, did not grow old. I suppose she was a hypocrite in her own small way, but she wasn't like everyone else who threw the Ten Commandments at me all the time and then went off to drink themselves into a reality where the lies by which they lived were sanctified by the precious metal they stripped from the golden rule—a rule they casually tossed into a landfill like an old television that didn't work anymore. Mrs. Fletcher was the kind of person who refused to be defined by the size of her television screen. She was the kind of person who simply lied a bit less than anyone else.

One time, I remember I was showing her how well I practiced my guitar scales. I was playing in the key of G. She stopped me with an abrupt thought. I stopped, hoping for a compliment.

Instead, she just asked, "How many times have you been told to grow up and act like an adult?"

I was fifteen at the time, and I knew about algebra and pi and multiplying by powers of whatever, so I figured it was something like that. That's what I told her. I asked if this was some kind of mathematical word problem.

She laughed and said, "No. That's not what I meant. I only thought to say that the very next time some old person points a finger and tells you to grow up— just ask what part of growing up is so important."

I nodded.

She wasn't finished.

"Ask them what part. Then ask if they mean the greedy part? Or the nuclear weapon part? Or the World War whatever part? Or vanity? Or pollution? Or the racist part? Ask them that."

"Sure," I said. Suddenly my sixteenth birthday didn't sound that great.

"Oh. Don't worry. It doesn't *have* to be that way."

Then she handed me the guitar part she had transcribed. "This will show you how to play Paul Simon's 'America.' It's very lovely. Please. It's a favorite of mine. Will you learn this?"

IN HOPE OF RAIN

"Of course," I said. I wanted to learn anything she gave me.

She handed me two more pieces. "Give these to Lydia. You see her every day."

"What are they?"

Mrs. Fletcher laughed. "You know Lydia. One is the piano music for a Phil Ochs song, 'I Ain't Marching Anymore.' The other is the guitar part for the Who's 'Won't Get Fooled Again.'"

"Why can't I play these?"

She glanced at me and said, "Because you don't like to yell, and she does." It was that simple. It was always that simple. I just didn't like to yell.

One more thing: As the three of us — Liddy, Belle, and I — stood near Mrs. Fletcher's coffin, I distinctly heard her voice say, "You should marry Lydia." That's all it said. I knew that the dead never smile. I knew the dead do not speak. Dead people can't be matchmakers. I knew all of that, but I also know what I heard.

Of course, Lydia didn't hear it. Belle didn't hear it, either. But I did.

The voice told me to marry Lydia. I had always played any piece of music for that old woman. I had always tried to please her. I even told her I saw those names carved into the tree bark. This request was well beyond my joke book of an autobiography. I was very good at hiding my emotions. Now, Mrs. Fletcher wanted me to shed my armor, like some train running wide-open across America, and tell Lydia Meanad that I loved her. Lydia was passion personified. I was a clever laugh. We were so very different, so I merely planted a promise and hoped for rain.

Oleomargarine and a
Vietnamese Guy
who could Sing

A WEEK AFTER THE FUNERAL, I went to pay a visit to Mrs. Fletcher. Now there were three stones to touch. I still wondered about that voice and smile. Belle was there, too. A coincidence, I suppose. In my life, I have found many coincidences. I have even believed a few events to be beyond the random collision of tiny matter in the universe. Belle was there, and she wasn't alone. She stood next to a guy we all called Moses.

That wasn't his real name.

Moses shook my hand, which was a decent thing to do. I knew Moses because we had been in a band together. I was sixteen at the time, and the group needed a guitarist because Jonathan Maenad, Lydia and Belle's brother, had decided he didn't like playing long-winded, progressive rock songs. Jonathan, apparently, wanted to play short songs with noise and energy. He wrote a song called "Serfing USA" that was recorded and played on local radio quite a bit. It caused the powers that reigned supreme in the local business world to raise a cautionary eyebrow because the song was a diatribe against selling one's soul to the material world—that very same world populated by those who took the gold from the golden rule and tossed the rest into the landfill where the gulls could peck away at the waste.

OLEOMARGARINE & A VIETNAMESE GUY
WHO COULD SING

Poor Jonathan became the stuff to fill a landfill. Local businessmen smelled money and pumped high octane booze into the guy so he would sing his protest song for them whenever they wanted it. Some people said this was their way of squashing such thoughts of protest. Who knows? Perhaps the big money in our town bought Jonathan's revolution and mounted it next to its bowling and softball trophies.

Perhaps Jonathan liked all the fame and liquor.

Anyway, Lydia and Belle's dear brother became a burned-out kid who, from time to time, signed an autograph in memory of his fifteen minutes of fame. There is, as I write this, an autographed photo of him hanging in the local liquor store next to photos of famous high school football stars from the local schools.

Did I mention Moses was Vietnamese? He was a Vietnamese guy who could sing well. So, he was in our group. We called ourselves A Warped Window? The idea was to have a name like The Doors, which was taken from *Doors of Perception*, a book by Aldous Huxley. I thought A Warped Window? was a really great name. Unfortunately, when we put signs all over town to advertise the group, most calls were from people who wanted to know how much we would charge to replace their windows or do other odd construction jobs.

We did manage to play a show here and there. It was all right with me because the music was cosmic spacey stuff that didn't really require any outpouring of emotional notes from my guitar. I could hide behind a smile that pretended to know the secrets of the universe.

Quite frankly, the others in the band were a bunch of potheads who only seemed to nod quite a bit whenever I talked to them. Moses was the token Asian singer. There was a band we liked called Can, who had Damo Suzuki, a Japanese singer, who sang about everyone's need for vegetable soup. We listened to their *Tago Mago* all the time. Moses was our bid for international progressive-rock fame.

Moses never smoked any dope, and the rest of the band never offered it to him. The rest of the band never even bothered to learn his real name.

One time, I suggested the band try a bit of real rock music. I played them a riff stolen from Led Zeppelin, who probably took it from some old blues guy: a blues guy who no adoring Robert Plant fan would even recognize if he happened to show up at a Zeppelin concert.

Well, I played this bit of rock music, and they all looked at me like I was from another planet, which was odd, because I thought that was the exact point of their jammed-out space music. The keyboard player sat on the floor of our practice room with his ear propped against the side panel of the small refrigerator. He had always made a big deal out of the fact that, apparently, the constant refrigerator hum was in the key of D-flat, which he claimed was the exact key of all true and pure vibrations on Mother Earth. This, too, was odd, because, for crying out loud, the guy was grooving to the constant hum of a compressor in a refrigerator made by General Electric! I guess this was just a sign of the times.

Like I said, the band didn't really require any emotional commitment. One day, I brought in a song and told the band it was called "White Gold." It was all about smuggling this "white gold" across "the border." The keyboard player, who was still listening to the refrigerator compressor hum, nodded in deep respect. I think his nose twitched several times like he was about to sneeze, but he didn't sneeze at all. That was just his way of approving what he thought was a tune with a hidden drug meaning.

OLEOMARGARINE & A VIETNAMESE GUY
WHO COULD SING

You see, that was all the rage then—ten out of ten on the youth culture's hip-o-meter. All sorts of people, both young and old, were sniffing through every song on the radio for hidden drug references cleverly disguised so they could be played on the commercial airwaves.

I did the unthinkable: I wrote a harmless song about oleomargarine, a well-known butter substitute. It was a song that just sounded like it was a paean to the land of the perpetual pipe dream. Let's face facts: "Puff the Magic Dragon" wasn't merely about a dragon named Puff. "Lucy in the Sky with Diamonds" made clever use of the letters LSD. The Stones song "Get Off of My Cloud" wasn't talking about any particular piece of real-estate with a "no trespassing" sign. Honestly, my contribution to the band was a song about oleomargarine, that well-known butter substitute. Of course, hipsters far and wide thought they knew the truth: They were certain "White Gold" was a wink and a smuggler's smile whispering the words "illegal substances" to anyone under, say, thirty years of age.

Well, they were right—but for the wrong reason. That drug bit was just another disguise that concealed the real sordid story: Oleomargarine was illegal in the state of Wisconsin until 1967. We Wisconsinites had for years flaunted the law and had knowingly carried this oleo contraband, this white gold, this well-known butter substitute, across state lines. We had even failed to heed our own dairy defender, W.D. Hoard, as he pleaded for "self-respecting men to take up the cudgels for the cow and defend her time-honored prerogatives."

Good for him!

But shame on us! Shame on my parents, who hid the butter substitute in the trunk of their Dodge as they passed the state police border patrol—and smiled with an innocent wave. Shame on Mrs. Anderson, our next-door neighbor, who once brought us a box of the illegal stuff she had bought in Michigan.

The song was a satirical finger pointed right between the eyes of middle-class, law-abiding, suburbia-living America. Not only that, the Vietnam War raged every night on our television sets as we smuggled this oleo. We watched while we ate our family dinner with our eyes glued to the scenes of death in some country that only seemed to exist in the twelve-inch screen of the black-and-white kitchen TV while we spread the illegal oleo on our family bread and flaunted democracy and its laws. Trust me: My song had nothing to do with drugs of any sort. It was just a song about oleomargarine, that well-known butter substitute.

Did I mention that Moses was a Vietnamese guy who could sing? He stood next to Belle and held her hand. She held his hand. He was still a bit of a rarity in our area. He was part of the first influx of war-torn refugees making its presence known on the landscape of our Green Bay Midwestern America.

For the most part, these Vietnamese people kept their distance. They kept their distance as they all ate together at their tables in our school cafeteria. They kept their distance as they bought their groceries in the local supermarkets. They kept their distance from any church I attended—and we kept our Christian distance.

Moses was different.

He sang in our band. He blended into our Caucasian culture quite well. We called him Moses because no one could pronounce his real name—not that any of us ever tried. The name Moses seemed to be good enough. We liked him, and we liked that name. We all liked him so well we figured he must have a vein of good old America in his gene pool supplied by some lonely G.I. who didn't have a clue why many Vietnamese spoke French so well.

OLEOMARGARINE & A VIETNAMESE GUY
WHO COULD SING

You know, we never even *tried* to pronounce his name. It was probably a racist thing, but he was happy that we called him Moses and let him sing in our band.

"So, who's going to take care of old Otis now?" Belle asked.

I didn't answer. I looked at their tightly held hands. There really wasn't much of a difference in their fingers. I thought for a moment she was probably a little embarrassed, and I shouldn't look. Now, of course, I realize I was wrong. She wasn't embarrassed at all. Belle didn't care if I looked at their intertwined fingers. I said, "I have Otis now. I promised her." I glanced toward Mrs. Fletcher's grave. "It's the least I can do."

Belle looked at Moses and asked, "Remember? I told you Otis was Mrs. Fletcher's dog."

"That's the dog who loves the old trees," Moses said. He didn't have an accent. That always surprised me. Vietnamese refugees didn't have an accent in their English. French people have an accent. German people have an accent. People from Alabama have an accent, but Moses and his Vietnamese friends spoke such soft and natural English.

"We all love those trees," Belle added.

"He'll spend most of the day there if I let him," I said.

"Just watching the world?" she asked.

"Sure. He and I just watch the world as it goes by."

"Does Otis laugh at your jokes?"

"No," I said slowly. "But I always laugh at the things he says. That old basset has a great sense of humor."

She smiled. "I guess he is a funny old basset hound." She paused for a moment. Then she said, "Take care of the old guy. He's all we have left. We want to keep all those trees."

She gave me a hug. Belle was a lovely person. She's still a lovely person, but her laugh doesn't dance with sabers anymore.

I watched as Belle and Moses slowly walked away. They were still holding hands.

At one time, I thought she was so different from her passionate protester of a sister. She was just as much a rebel, but hers was a quiet and perhaps even a happy rebellion. Her rebellion did not contain many words but was filled with that razor laugh, and her rebellion held the hand of a Vietnamese guy—a Vietnamese guy who could sing well and didn't have an accent in his English.

blame it on
Zorro
the Hamster

AFTER MRS. FLETCHER DIED, I went through a period of, let's just say, extreme sarcasm. I think old Otis egged me on as we sat together between the two old oak trees and made fun of the world all around us. I know. It sounds silly to suggest an old basset hound could, as I said, egg me past the point of mere observation and into a world of social commentary; but take my word for it, old Otis was much more humorous than I could ever hope to be. Sure, he couldn't talk. He just barked and panted, but he was a natural comedian.

I just talked.

I think we met somewhere in the middle.

In my extreme sarcasm, I even included the two huge oak trees between which Otis and I sat. I spoke to them. They were old and beautiful, and everyone knew those trees. They were Eloise and Noah. So Otis and I included them in our conversation. It just seemed like the appropriate thing to do.

There's nothing wrong with talking to trees.

I was sent to see a psychiatrist. I think, in an odd way, my parents thought it was also the appropriate thing to do. After all, I was eighteen. They were concerned as they watched me, their only son, laugh out loud while I sat between two old oak trees and talked to a dog. It really didn't bother me when they made the appointment. Sarcastic people can usually see everybody else's point of view.

Sadly, Old Otis couldn't go with me. I was on my own.

The psychiatrist's name was Dr. Rein. I thought her name would be pronounced with the same vowel sound as in the word "mean." But no, it rhymed with Cain, the Biblical guy who killed his brother. That was not a good omen. I had an English teacher in high school, Miss Turnkee, who taught us all about symbolism. Rein was not necessarily a good thing. The rhyming with Cain didn't help the situation. The couch in her office was the same leather used for fighter pilots' flight jackets. I think it's called stressed leather. That wasn't a good sign either.

"Would you like a cup of coffee?" she asked.

"Sure," I said, somewhat sarcastically. "I like it so strong and thick that famous Hollywood types try to leave their hand and footprints and sign their names in it."

She returned with the coffee. "I'll send out for Chinese food if you like. Then you and your coffee will be right at home." She smiled. Old Otis would have liked her.

Dr. Rein read over some file somebody prepared for my session. I was a bit surprised because she already had quite a few pages to review. "So," she said slowly. "You seem to have a problem with anger."

"That's one way of looking at it," I answered.

"All right. What's another way of looking at it?" She hit the ball back into my court.

"Well," I confessed. "The only problem I have with anger is that I never seem to get angry."

"Everybody gets angry."

"I don't."

"Why not?"

I thought for several moments. I wanted to tell her about the gravestones with three names on them, but I didn't trust her that much. That was none of her business. "I guess," I tried to explain, "I'm too busy laughing to get mad."

"Laughing at what?"

"Everything."

"Everything?" She raised an eyebrow—just like Otis raised an eyebrow.

"Everything except Otis and Noah and Eloise."

"Are they your friends?"

I thought for a second and then answered. "That's one way of looking at it."

She raised the other eyebrow. "So what's another way of looking at it?"

She was a good tennis player. So I served an honest answer right back at her. "Well, one's a dog and the other two are trees."

She paused. Then she checked her notes. For some reason, I wished I had notes to check. I felt sort of naked. Naked wasn't good. She glanced up from her reading. "Tell me about your childhood."

"It was intense." That's all I said.

"Intense?" That's all she said.

I said absolutely nothing.

"Why was it so intense?"

"Why is anything intense?"

She thought for a few seconds. "Is that the reason you laugh all the time?"

"No."

"So what do you do instead of laugh?"

"Instead?"

BLAME IT ON ZORRO THE HAMSTER

"Yes, what do you do?"

"Instead of laughing?" I asked.

"Yes, what do you do?"

I decided to be honest. "I guess I just don't laugh."

She wrote that down.

"That is," I said, "if not laughing is something you can do."

"That's an interesting question."

"That's one way of looking at it," I answered. Then I laughed. Otis would have chuckled, too. I thought of telling her about Debbie. But it just wasn't her business. So I told her about Zorro instead. "Zorro made me laugh," I said.

"Zorro? Like the guy in the mask?"

"No. Zorro, like the pet hamster we had in the third-grade classroom. He had black circles around his eyes, so we called him Zorro." That made sense.

"How did Zorro make you laugh?"

"He died," I said.

"That was funny?"

"No." I thought for a moment. "I felt bad he died. It's just the teacher made such a big deal to lie about the whole thing. The way I figured it, there are other hamsters looking for a cage in a classroom. But we had to sit in a big circle, and Miss Gallagher was teary-eyed and told us that Zorro had gone to 'a much better place than this.'

"I looked around the classroom and just honestly said, 'You'll have to be much more specific. That could be just about any-where.' That was the start. Everybody else was so sad. I just felt she needed to be more specific.

"A few kids laughed. Then they weren't so sad. I simply wanted to make more kids less sad."

Dr. Rein checked her notes. She said, "It says here your

third-grade report card stated that you drew birds really well." She paused and added, "It says that you were too sincere for your age. What happened? So when did sincerity turn to sarcasm?"

"I guess you have to blame it on Zorro the hamster."

"So it was Zorro and then the drugs?"

"What drugs?"

She checked those notes again.

"It says here that you wrote a song called 'White Gold' about smuggling drugs across the border. Apparently, you were quite famous in the area. Did these drugs have anything to do with the change in your personality?"

"That song wasn't about drugs."

"No?"

"It was about oleomargarine."

She gave me a strange look. "You mean the well-known butter substitute?"

"Well, it may be just a butter substitute to you, but it was illegal contraband to the Wisconsin State Patrol. Gordon Roseleip, who was a big-time state politician, wanted it to be dyed red because he thought it was a communist plot."

"Butter was illegal?"

"No, oleomargarine was illegal."

"Why?"

"We're a dairy state. Dairy cows can't make oleo."

"So you smuggled it into the state?"

"Well, my parents brought it in. We hid it in the trunk, under the blankets."

Dr. Rein took a moment to write several notes in my file. "Let's see, then," she said. "You're here because you have a prob-lem with anger?"

"That's right."

BLAME IT ON ZORRO THE HAMSTER

"But you never get angry."

"That's right."

"You are sarcastic."

"That's right."

"And your drug song wasn't really about drugs at all."

"That's right."

"It was about oleomargarine."

"That's right. It was about an illegal well-known butter substitute."

"And some guy thought oleo was a communist plot."

"That's right. He wanted to color the stuff red."

"How about the bird drawings in third grade?"

"What do you want to know?"

"Were they as good as the report card says?"

"I suppose so. I mean I could draw a bird for you right now if you want me to do it."

"Would I be impressed?" she asked.

I thought for a moment. "Probably not. I mean it would be decent for a little kid, but it would be cruddy for, you know, an eighteen-year-old. I just haven't gotten any better."

"That doesn't bother you?"

"Not really. I never really wanted to draw birds."

"Did you want to draw Zorro?"

She was good. Her question hit close to my heart. I wanted to draw Debbie — a Debbie with no hair — a Debbie staring at me while I glanced at Jesus hanging on the cross. But I kept my mouth shut. There was a cancerous silence.

"I'm sorry," she said. "I really don't see any problems here."

"Problems?"

"Yes," she said. "I don't really find any problems."

Then I simply said, "There's a big problem."

"What's that?" she asked.

I was blunt. "Otis is old. When he dies, they're going to cut down Noah and Eloise and all the other trees. They're going to build a big apartment complex where all the trees used to be. Otis is the only thing that stands in their way. He's so old. Bassets just don't live long enough. Once he's gone, they can do anything they want."

She wrote something in her notebook.

I just said, "I have to save those trees."

She wrote a bit more.

Then I laughed. Well, in truth, I probably went on and on about old Otis, Mrs. Fletcher, and all the trees. Dr. Rein took all sorts of notes, and as I told her more about those trees, she took more notes and nodded several times. Finally, she dropped the notepad, looked at me, and said one final thing. She simply said, "We're in big trouble."

Then she stopped writing, and our session was over.

a Reagan Rally

LET'S SEE: I HAD BEEN TO A GRAVEYARD; I had been to see a psychiatrist; and I needed to finish the hat trick with a stop at a local bar, a place called The Spirit of '76 Proof. I wanted to see a local band, a band that had a different name every time they played. They made an album when they were known as Foghat Cancelled. That night, as I recall, the marquee simply read, "Reagan Rally."

I was surprised. There were many people with signs who were waiting to get into the Spirit of '76 Proof. Their signs told the world that Ronald Wilson Reagan was their choice to be President of the United States. Their signs called Jimmy Carter, the current president, all sorts of nasty names. I was surprised there were so many people and so much press. I think they expected a political rally; but really, it was all about a band that happened to call itself Reagan Rally for the evening.

As I sat in my car and thought about the possibility of Ronald Reagan being elected as the next President of the United States, for some reason I also thought about all the things I had not told Dr. Rein. Sure, she knew about old Otis, Noah, and Eloise, but I had not told her the rest of the story.

How could I explain to a complete stranger everything I

felt about trees and music? How could I tell her I cared about these things? This was inside stuff, deep inside stuff—Monroe Doctrine stuff—hands off and don't tread on me stuff.

How could I tell her about Debbie? She would never hear Mrs. Fletcher playing her guitar as she urged all of us to love music. This old woman had never sold her soul. She knew how to be young a lot better than we did. "Live between the moments of your life," she would say, "and play music between the notes. Debussy said that. Listen to the sea. Listen to his music. Watch a fawn just a moment before its afternoon begins. Then remember everything that never happened. Play music and listen as it disappears." She paused and then softly said, "Don't ever give your soul away."

I was just a kid, but I knew enough to avoid Faustus' fate.

Call it instinct.

Call it grace.

Call me Ishmael.

Call me a fool.

I once asked, "But where does it go?" I was talking about music, but the question held a much greater begging bowl. I suppose gravestones are necessary to prove someone was alive: *I have a gravestone. Therefore, I once was.* The inverse, of course, may also be true: *I don't have a gravestone. Therefore, I am. Therefore, I beg.*

"From whence it comes." That's all she said. She sounded old and poetic, like a Bob Dylan song still played after 200 years. Her words seemed like a reasonable answer, so I didn't beg with any more questions.

Did we understand all of this stuff? Probably not. I'm not certain I do today. I remember the dim lights of the funeral parlor. Mrs. Fletcher was impossibly quiet while she lay in that coffin. She was like the space between the notes Debussy described in his music—the sound of the leaves drifting in the gentle air. She reminded me of some ancient Egyptian mummy filled with secrets and sandy dust.

I remember the day I approached her gravestone for the first time. Belle and Moses were there, holding hands. Belle read the name. She confessed she never knew Mrs. Fletcher's first name was Thecla. That was the name inscribed on the tombstone: Thecla Fletcher. It was so definite. She once was.

I told Belle it was a family name. Of course, Belle, as she always did, asked to know more. She always expected something more than what was given to her.

I told her it was a Biblical name. Thecla was a woman who traveled with Paul, and they both preached the Gospel and gave communion. They both knew the ascetic life. Belle said she knew of St. Paul, but she didn't know about a woman named Thecla. I explained that some pope didn't like Thecla because women weren't supposed to preach the Gospel, so he literally wrote her out of the story. Belle wondered how he could do that. She thought the Gospel was different from a comic book, or a detective story, or a daily soap opera where characters were easily written out of the plot. Belle said the Bible couldn't be changed.

She said the Bible was too true to be changed.

Mrs. Fletcher had told me about the name, and the woman, and the pope who erased Thecla from history. Then I told Belle I was really happy comics could be changed. Captain America died, but then they brought him back to life. I think that was the right thing to do, even if it was only possible in a comic book.

A REAGAN RALLY

So, how can I explain about the trees?

Well, as we stood in front of Mrs. Fletcher's grave, Belle suggested we plant a tree to shade the spot. Moses said he didn't think it was possible to plant a tree in a cemetery. I told them that it was a shame if so—because Mrs. Fletcher had loved her trees as they watched the world go by.

As I have said, the trees had names, Noah and Eloise, both planted by Mrs. Fletcher's grandparents on their first wedding anniversary. There were others with names. Their first child, Thecla, was named for the rebellious woman. She was our Mrs. Fletcher's aunt. Noah planted the tree that bore her name on the day she was born. Sadly, Thecla lived the forgotten life of her Biblical namesake. She married a man whose only vow was to his own ego. He left his wife to a sad story of her own.

There were other trees because Noah and Eloise had four more children. Paul, who was a pilot—and probably named for the saint—died in the Great War. I have seen some sepia photos of Paul standing in front of his Neuport aeroplane. He is smiling in the photograph. His brother, Daniel, died an infant. His tree grew tall, planted next to the oak that bore Thecla's name. Erna, a sister, contracted tuberculosis. She was sent to live away from the family and never returned. Poor Erna never had a proper youth. Prayers, of course, were offered. Divine aid was invoked. Bible stories are nice in their own way, but Erna was unable to sling even one rock at her Goliath of an illness.

I was told Erna waved as she was being taken away.

She waved and she smiled.

Packages were sent to her with photos and gifts. Once, the family received a sincere letter from a worker at the sanitarium telling them the stuffed dog they sent was, in the best of ways, her only friend. The letter said Erna never lost her sense of humor, even as the disease gained its towering command. The letter said Erna always laughed, and she was not defined by her illness because her laugh was just too strong. In the end, Erna could not sleep because in her illness, she believed the dog to be real, and she worried that her dog couldn't run and be free outside. She also fretted over the fact that all dogs need to go to the bathroom, and in her hospital room, there was no place for a dog to do that. It was a kind letter saying she prayed every night.

Erna's disease could not stop her gentle concern for the world. Goliath could stop only her heart; he could not change its nature. St. Francis with his stigmata never managed to laugh at tuberculosis like Erna did, and he never cared so passionately for a stuffed dog. Erna was far from sainthood, but she was never a victim of this life. Sometimes I like to think her laugh is heard as the wind moves through the branches of her namesake tree.

Another brother, Peter, was never meant to be a pilot, and instead charged out of trenches when he was told to charge out of those trenches and was lucky enough to outlive the war to end all wars. All of Noah and Eloise's children had trees to bear their names, as did Peter and his wife, Lily, and their only son, Simon, who most assuredly never signed the treaty at Versailles but was sadly asked to pay its reparations as he stumbled onto Normandy Beach.

He was wet and exhausted and without his rifle. His landing craft had stuck itself into a sandbar, and he had to swim to shore. He just continued to stumble forward until someone told him the war was over. Unfortunately, his battle wasn't over for very long; he was called up for the Korean conflict. When he returned home, this veteran of two wars wanted nothing more than to avoid another battle and enjoy the Eden of his own backyard garden. He did.

But his son, Franklin Michael, lost his college deferment and left for Vietnam as his parents cried on their doorstep. He was a decent kid when he left. He was not particularly kind or unkind, or smart or ambitious, but he came back changed. He didn't hate the world, he didn't drink, and he didn't mention post-traumatic problems. He simply hated things that grew and had leaves.

Franklin called it all "the jungle." He wanted to destroy that jungle. That, of course, put him on a collision course with his Aunt Thecla, our Mrs. Fletcher, the younger sister of Simon. Franklin had war in his eyes, yet no one cared to see that war. Everyone simply wanted an excuse to avoid the look in his eyes.

His Aunt Thecla—our Mrs. Fletcher—understood about Franklin's fears. She never avoided the look in her nephew's eyes. She never avoided the look in anybody's eyes.

That's why I always listened and learned from the music of Mrs. Fletcher's words. That's why I wanted to make other people laugh. Sure, she was human. But her humanity built such a lean diet of a façade—the thinnest I have even known. Any wolf could blow his way right through it. Mrs. Fletcher never worried about those wolves. So the wolves never bothered her and stayed far away.

Lydia, a damsel distressed by the world, with short skirts, tights, and high-topped tennis shoes, was a frequent visitor to the world within those weak walls. I was a visitor, too, a joker whose only armor was the sarcastic comment and a good laugh. Yeah, that's why I loved that old woman. She said things that weren't meant to be humorous. She never lied to me.

Just about everything is a lie; just about everything is an excuse, an excuse to avoid the accusatory faces of soldiers with war in their eyes who hoped for a reprieve, an excuse to avoid the glances of young people who figured out the truth — a truth that said no reprieve was in the offing for their generation.

Mrs. Fletcher was blunt and honest and human. She was a good piece of literature I wanted to read. She was a lovely piece of music I desperately wanted to play. She was a teacher who never bothered with the curriculum of being a teacher. She was an aged mother who never stopped loving the world — simply because her child needed to live in that world.

This old woman was acutely aware of the deception that creeps about this world — even in Eden. There is always a man behind the curtain: He may be a wizard in Oz, or he may be sweet Ophelia's fool of a father. He may be the guy who types the draft notices for any current war. It's all the same.

Lydia and Belle's brother Jonathan sang a song called "Serfing USA." It was a warning about selling your soul to bankers and business people. It was a good song, but unfortunately, the man behind the curtain gave poor Jonathan too much booze, and he became a joke with a punch line about as humorous as a liver drowning in a sea of vodka. Jonathan and his song were just another Titanic that hit a different iceberg.

All sorts of people showed up for Reagan Rally. Of course, there was no promise that Ronald Reagan, the Republican candidate for president in 1980, would be there. All people saw was a sign that read, "Reagan Rally." They were ready. They were ready in red, white, and blue; they were ready with streamers; and they were ready with firecrackers, even though the Fourth of July had morphed into early August.

A REAGAN RALLY

There was a sign that read, "It's Morning in America!" Another proudly proclaimed, "We Are Not Better Off Than We Were Four Years Ago!" Some signs weren't that clever. They simply stated: "Reagan in '80!" "Reagan for President!" and "Win One for the Gipper!"

The other side was there, too, of course. Lydia was standing with a sign that read, "Save the Trees and the Sandinistas!" I noticed her blond dreadlocks as she stood with all her friends. She knew so many people who protested everything. To be honest, their side looked a lot like the minutemen eagerly awaiting Paul Revere. The Reagan people just looked like they were ready for a good time—about eight years of a good time.

The odd thing was there really was no rally. I knew this. Reagan Rally was the name used by this band that changed their name all the time. The group had been on the local scene long enough to make at least one record, which, naturally, didn't sell well at all; but I liked the group, and I bought their album. It had a long song called "We Came in Peace for All Mankind," which is the message written on the plaque we Americans left on the moon. Their song questioned the accuracy of this claim. Thinking about the Fletcher family's affiliation with all the wars of the last century, I suppose the band had a point, and I understood the humor. But honest! I was just there to see the band that happened to call itself Reagan Rally. The others were there to duke... or perhaps Dutch it out.

There was one other sign that proclaimed: "Cut Me Down Before I Kill Again!" The guy who held it was Henry Thumm. I knew him from school. Henry was a practicing Greek Mythologist who told everyone he had an altar to Poseidon in his parents' basement. Henry petitioned our school board to move the study of Greek mythology into the science classes because, to him, the gods were as real as anything Darwin or the Bible ever suggested. The idea proved to be a nonstarter, but that was our Henry Thumm with that sign.

I waved.

Henry waved back.

All of Mrs. Fletcher's trees knew Henry Thumm, too. I should mention there was one tree having no name at all, yet it was accepted as part of the family. Somebody suggested it was planted for a possible miscarriage, while others thought it stood for everyone else who loved nature. Henry claimed this unnamed tree was in keeping with his own beliefs as a practicing Greek Mythologist. He claimed each Greek town set up an altar to the "unknown god," just in case one had been missed.

I agreed with Henry. It's never a good idea to miss a god.

I remembered Mrs. Fletcher told me about the scars on Noah and Eloise. She had me touch those scars by rubbing my fingers against the bark. Of course, I made a sarcastic remark about Saint Thomas putting his fingers in the wounds of Christ. She didn't laugh, and neither did I. It really wasn't a very good joke. A bad joke is like any kid's death in a war or a shirt made in Vietnam's sweatshops and sold in America.

"Can you feel the letters?" she earnestly asked.

"The letters?"

"They are there."

"Why did they carve them?"

"Because they were in love. People in love defy the universe. He carved her name, and she carved his name." I touched one of the trees again, and she asked, "Do you see the names?"

I didn't say a word.

"You're a good boy," she said. "You don't want to hurt my feelings. They are there. That's what nature does. It is so much more patient than we are. Think how long a star has to wait for us to see its light. Yet it still continues to shine. Those trees have the names scratched in their bark. Those trees have taken those words and moved them closer, every year, to the very center of their hearts. Those names are still there. Trust me. They are still there. They are etched into the very souls of these old oaks. Noah has Eloise, and Eloise has her Noah. "I gently touched each tree for a third time.

I was thinking back to the day I touched those trees as I parked my car in the lot at the Spirit of '76 Proof. I thought about the names carved into those oaks. I also thought about those strange words Mrs. Fletcher somehow said while I stood in front of her coffin. I was to marry Liddy. Sure. Liddy was to marry me. Sure, again.

I looked into the big crowd. There was my Liddy, dressed in a dark blue skirt with green tights. She always wore dresses and tights, and her lovely blond dreadlocks punched back and forth like a boxer as she yelled something at someone else who just happened to have a "Reagan for President" sign.

My Liddy—I glanced at her. She was still yelling. Her blond dreadlocks were flailing through the air. Wow! Could she yell!

I desperately wanted to say something sarcastic. For some reason, I just hummed a bit of that Paul Simon song, "America"—the one Mrs. Fletcher wanted me to learn. I didn't do the tune justice because I never sang, but I hummed the song anyway. Why not? I was ready to go and see my favorite band, known tonight as Reagan Rally.

The band played all of my favorites. Music had changed so

much from the heyday of progressive rock in 1974. Since that time, punk, disco, and reggae had shortened things up a bit. Most of the big bands couldn't get away with album-length epics anymore. A few of the bands, like Genesis, lost a lead singer and gained a hit single. Reagan Rally, or whatever their name happened to be on a given night, wasn't any different. They played everything really fast and loud. The audience loved it and danced in the aisles. One guy stood perfectly still until the first quick note. Then he jumped and flopped around like he had just ingested a loaf of bread laced with ergot.

When the music stopped, the guy stood frozen, in that moment, without a Beach Boy good vibration.

I never did figure out if he was a Reagan supporter.

I was a fan of the band. At first, I was a little disappointed at the acceleration of their songs. I quickly realized they were just playing their old long songs faster and stopping every three minutes. They were very precise. Each song stopped exactly three minutes after it began. There would be a pause, just like the space between songs on an album. Then, they would start again, but it was just a continuation of the same long song. They played the entire thirty-minute version of "We Came in Peace for All Mankind." The audience appeared happy enough because they did not desire to sit through long-winded, epic-length songs about traveling into space. They applauded after each neatly trimmed three-minute segment of the epic-length progressive-rock song about traveling into space.

The guy next to me, who had a Reagan campaign button pinned to his tie, looked at me. He shouted, "This is a great band for this rally! Every song is short!"

I nodded in agreement.

He shouted, "One time, I had to sit through a band playing all

A REAGAN RALLY

really long songs. I kept falling asleep! You know what I mean?"

I nodded in agreement again.

"I work for an investment firm, and I make all kinds of money! But it's the same thing! We have big meetings, but when they get too long, I just doze off! You know what I mean?"I nodded again and looked at his Reagan campaign button stuck in his tie. It was dark in the bar, but the tie looked like it was red, white, and blue.

The lead singer of Reagan Rally disappeared for a moment and then reappeared with a large cardboard cutout. As he turned it around, the crowd cheered. It was a life-sized cardboard photo of Ronald Reagan, the man who stood not only as a cardboard effigy on the stage, but also as a man on the precipice of being elected as the next President of the United States.

The photo they had used was taken from the future commander-in-chief's stint as the Twenty Mule Team Borax pitchman on *Death Valley Days*. The crowd cheered. Some, I believe, cheered because they loved Reagan, while some others cheered because they saw the cardboard cutout as a bit of a joke. I guess everyone paid money, and they had each made their choice. We get to do that in America. We get to do that with every president.

The lead singer put his arm around the cardboard Ronald Reagan like they were old war buddies. "This next song," he said, "this next song is a brand-new one. It was written by The Clap—our guitarist. He wrote it just for tonight."

The Clap laughed and explained, "You know, originally this song was called 'Death Valley Days Are Here Again.'" He paused. Then he explained a bit more. "But I saw this guy outside with a sign saying something about killing a tree before it murders again. Yeah. You know what that's about, don't you? The next president said trees cause more air pollution than cars."

"So," the lead singer suggested, "let's cut down more trees

and build more automobiles. That makes sense to me!"

The guy next to me wearing the Reagan campaign button said, "Ronnie's going to be a great president! You know what I mean? He rides horses and cuts wood. He was a big hero in the war in some film. You know what I mean? Yeah! Cut the trees and stop pollution. You know what I mean? Reagan for more cars and fewer trees!"

"Well," The Clap said, "one time people wanted to cut those big redwoods in California, and Reagan, let's see, he was governor then, said if you've seen one redwood tree, then you've seen them all. Well, I've just changed the name of the song. It was called 'Death Valley Days Are Here Again,' but now it's called 'A Tree Might Just Be a Tree, But a Crouton Is Not Always a Crouton.' The song has nothing at all to do with Ronald Reagan. It's got absolutely nothing to do with America or the election. It's about Croutons." He paused. "But just in case you are concerned, it has very little to do with salads and salad dressing."

The Clap was right on, as we used to say.

The song, which exceeded the three-minute mark by some distance, was all about a race of aliens called Croutons. These aliens called Croutons had the habit of eavesdropping on radio signals from just about everywhere in the universe. These Croutons were just like us — except they went to mass on Tuesday, they celebrated Easter in January, and on their birthdays, it was their practice to give presents to close friends for putting up with stupidity for yet another year — which in Crouton time lasted approximately 52,765 of our days. They simply felt it was the decent thing to do because that was a long time to tolerate stupidity — even from the best of companions.

One day, these Croutons accidentally intercepted a portion

A REAGAN RALLY

of a Julia Childs' cooking show during which she whipped up several varieties of salads — salads including a number of things like mushrooms, tomatoes, cucumbers, cheese, lettuce, and of course, croutons. That's the only word they heard! Croutons! Croutons! They were Croutons! Croutons were being eaten in these salads!

Thinking their own kind were being devoured, these Croutons, after much deliberation because they were fundamentally a democratic society like our own, decided to attack these Earthlings who ate these salads every day.

These Croutons, who felt themselves threatened, decided to invade Earth in a preemptive strike. They destroyed quite a bit of Earth because of the Julia Childs cooking show. According to the lyrics of the song, the Croutons destroyed two-thirds of the human population, and they leveled our greatest monuments, including Mount Rushmore, the Taj Mahal, the Library of Congress, the Eiffel Tower, and of course, Lambeau Field, the home of the Green Bay Packers football franchise. Even Vatican City was obliterated.

After all this destruction, the Croutons discovered their mistake. There was a huge difference between themselves and the crunchy bits of bread sprinkled into our salads every day. They felt really bad — as well they should! The Crouton aliens were pretty smart and felt some sort of obligation for their destruction.

But, let's face it: The Croutons knew they could not rebuild everything they destroyed, especially the Taj Mahal, which was a very beautiful building. So they hung around for a while and did the best they could under the circumstances. They said they were sorry. In fact, they said they were sorry several times. They even said they were disappointed. With their limited budget, they could build only a few factories in which the remaining humans could find work.

The Croutons also explained their idea of government and religion and then set up several of their restaurant chains that were not totally dissimilar to, say, McDonalds, Burger King, or Taco Bell, which existed en masse on our planet before it was destroyed by a preemptive mistake.

By the way, the actual lyrics to the song Reagan Rally played that night were written by a local poet and sometime short story writer named Jenny Ego. She wrote all the words to their songs. The Clap wrote the music. The fact that Jenny Ego had been credited as the song's lyric-writer has very little to do with this story. However, Jenny Ego, at this time, did own an Irish setter named Dara Ruthie Rose, which is important. I don't know if Jenny owned a dog of any kind in the year 2003, when America launched its own preemptive strike against Iraq.

The band played another song: my song, "White Gold." They probably meant it as a tribute. Heaven only knows. Let's face it. The song was popular because it sure sounded like one of those subversive drug songs. But really! It was just about oleomargarine, a well-known butter substitute that was illegal contraband in Wisconsin until 1967.

The band knew this. That was part of their fun. That was part of their tribute to me. I should really have been quite happy. The lead singer announced that Joshua Toss, the writer of the song, was in the audience. For some odd reason, I raised my hand.

The guy next to me, the guy with the Reagan campaign button stuck in his tie, looked me over. I felt a little bit dirty.

He kept looking at me. Finally, he said, "You wrote that?"

I nodded. I still felt dirty.

"Man," he said. "White gold, man, you know what I mean?"

I truly believe his nose twitched, just like that guy in A

A REAGAN RALLY

Warped Window? who had his head against the refrigerator and hummed the big note of Mother Earth.

"White gold," he said again. "You have any? You know what I mean?"

I played innocent. "Huh?"

"You know." His nose twitched again. "You got any white gold out in your car?"

"Sure," I said. I was thinking about the turkey sandwich I had stuffed under the front seat about three weeks ago. It was probably a whiter shade of mold by now.

"I'll pay top dollar," he said. "I work for an investment firm. You know what I mean? I make mega money." He fiddled with his Reagan campaign button.

"Sure thing," I said to him. "I'll be right back."

He looked at me with an intensity that was downright scary. "You're a rock star. You know what I mean? You're a rock star!"

"Yeah, I know." That's all I could think to say. I just walked outside with a certain sense of authority, and then I left. I just left. I thought about bringing the poor guy whatever was left of the turkey sandwich, but I didn't have that much sarcasm left inside of me. I thought about my bad St. Thomas joke and those lovely trees. I just wanted to go. I just wanted to go far away from the moment.

So that's what I did.

I just walked away.

As I walked to my car, I noticed Liddy, all alone, the very last protester still standing outside the bar. The final protester is always a sad sight. She still held her sign that said, "Save the Trees and the Sandinistas!" I had forgotten she was a year-and-a-half younger than everyone else. She was just seventeen and couldn't get into the bar.

THE GOSPEL ACCORDING TO DARA

She looked so sad.

I wanted to tell her a joke.

She had dead-soldier eyes. Those were lovely eyes. Those were ancient eyes.

I waved at her, but she didn't wave back.

the Big Bang Theory and a Garden Rake

OTIS AND I SAT TOGETHER and watched the cars go by in our neighborhood. Life can be quite simple. Trees and dogs, what more could anyone desire? Old Otis was in rare basset form. I sat next to him on one of the chairs between Noah and Eloise. They were beautiful old metal chairs that had been painted and repainted several times. Layers of the paint peeled like sunburned skin, with bits of yellow, blue, and orange. Those chairs looked like the sunset.

I gently picked a tune on my guitar. It was the melody from Paul Simon's "America."

Now, I don't want anyone to think that Otis was really being sarcastic. Of course not, but he was, indeed, in rare form. Mrs. Fletcher once told me to remember everything that didn't happen. Well, listening to Otis was something like that. I heard everything that wasn't said, or in this case, barked. Believe me, when the rich neighbors drove by in their fancy cars, Otis said absolutely nothing. He just looked at them in a certain way. Then when the neighbors who weren't rich but wanted so desperately to be rich drove by in their cars, Otis just looked at me with his sagging oval eyes. I knew exactly what he was thinking: Humans have invented language, dog treats, comfortable shoes, electricity, gardening, the flush toilet, the bicycle, central heating, the refrigerator, wool sweaters, the printing press, recorded music, penicillin, beer, and the comfortable bed. After that, everything is gratuitous.

Mr. Harper walked his usual route. He was a joyous old guy—a miracle—who had lived enough to enjoy the foolishness of this life. Mr. Harper always petted Otis' head. The two of them shared a laugh, and I was lucky enough to enjoy that laugh.

So, I just let Otis go on and on. Boy! That old dog was funny.

I played my guitar. I thought about all sorts of things. I thought about Belle and Moses. I thought about their hands. His hands were much darker than her hands. I thought about those weird words I had heard at Mrs. Fletcher's funeral—I should marry Lydia. I should marry Lydia with her long blond dreadlocks and high-topped tennis shoes.

Unfortunately, Lydia was mad at me. That's why she hadn't returned my wave, but it wasn't my fault.

Well, it wasn't *really* my fault.

I can't help being sarcastic. Perhaps my sarcasm is my weird way of showing affection. There should be a *Twilight Zone* episode where everyone is in love and gets to be sarcastic to one another. The audience could watch for twenty-five minutes and think they all hate each other, but in the ironic twisted ending, we can find out all the characters really love each other. I'd fit right into that world.

I had waved, but she hadn't waved back. I had told her that the sign she held that begged us to save the trees was probably made from the very trees she hoped to save, and she gave me one of her looks. It was the same look she gave me when I told her she had to sing songs by Captain and Tennille. It was a look saying she was tired of me. It was a look that hurt, a look that hurt like an insulting punch from a friend who knew the darkest secrets of your soul.

Dr. Rein suggested I think about my obvious lack of anger. This was nothing new. For some reason, I thought about those weird words I heard at Mrs. Fletcher's funeral, telling me to marry Lydia. I thought about those beautiful blond dreadlocks as they flayed at the universe in stubborn protest. I wanted to yell. Then Dr. Rein would pronounce me cured. Instead, I laughed. That was my answer. I wasn't happy with that answer, but it was all I had.

Dr. Rein also suggested I keep a journal, something psychiatrists always do. She was the expert, so that's what I did. I decided to make a few lists. Lists are always good. They create order.

The second list I decided to write was a history of punk rock music. Punk rock was music that came from anger, so I decided the list might help me. I thought about all this protest music—the stuff that Lydia really enjoyed, and that thought made me feel better. My words were a poem for her.

I told the world that William Blake invented punk music when he wrote a lyric called "London" that said everything Otis was able to suggest in a simple basset bark, even though old Otis had never been to England. That was punk rock. The Sex Pistols, in spite of their reputation, never spewed such spittle. Blake never played the Marquee, but read Blake's words. Read his "London." God save the Queen! God save the Kinks! Please, God save every Chimney Sweeper!

Next, I noted in my journal that Joseph "Papa" Haydn wrote a symphony called *The Surprise*. It was subtitled *Number 94*. It

THE BIG BANG THEORY AND A GARDEN RAKE

had a huge percussive big bang he hoped would blow the wigs off the rich women in the front rows, and it apparently did just that. It's a good thing to blow the wigs off people who really don't need to wear them.

There are so many others.

John Coltrane blew down the walls of Jericho with his music. Listen to his *Ascension*. Frank Zappa wrote *Lumpy Gravy*. The Good Rats, The Monks, The Ramones: they were all part of that big bang. Mott the Hoople wrote a song called "The Moon Upstairs." Listen to that, and listen to The MC5. Listen to The Stooges. Listen to Creedence Clearwater Revival's "Fortunate Son." Listen to Robert Johnson and Howlin' Wolf. For crying out loud! Listen to Little Richard and The Flamin' Groovies.

Peter Hammill wrote an album's worth of punky songs called *Nadir's Big Chance*. His songs, too, blew the wigs off the rich people. That's what music should do. Otis did this with his barking. That old dog, with his uncontrollable tuft, just blew the wigs off rich women who didn't need wigs. John Lennon told the wealthy people in the front row of a Beatles concert to rattle their jewelry. It's the same thing.

I stopped for a moment and looked at Otis. I thought about showing him more pictures of female dogs. He was the only hope. You see, he was all we had left.

Franklin, Mrs. Fletcher's nephew, who came home from Vietnam with an urgent itch to defoliate the world, wanted to cut down Noah, Eloise, Paul, Peter, Thecla, Erna, and any other tree that stood in his way. He wanted to turn this "nature piety" of our sacred spot into a high-rise apartment complex. Mrs. Fletcher stated in her final will and testament that the oak trees, now technically belonging to her nephew, could not be cut down until her old basset hound, Otis, or, "every descendant of that old basset known as Otis," had passed away.

So we needed Otis to sire a pup to save the trees. That pup could stop Franklin Fletcher from defoliating the world and allow the old memories to exist for a little more time to shade this earth for a few more years. Shade is a wonderful thing. A few memories might just manage to defy the marketplace of its profit, power, and control of everything.

One time, Mrs. Fletcher told me about her grandmother, Eloise, and a man named Stanley Goast. Stanley owned the big town factory and was smitten with the much younger Eloise. She refused him and married Noah instead. Well, Noah worked for Stanley Goast, and Stanley waited until Christmas to give every worker some sort of bonus. To Noah he gave nothing at all. Stanley Goast owned the factory, and he could do that. When Noah was fired, he and Eloise had precious little left, so Eloise took in the town's laundry.

One day, Stanley confronted her and tried to show her what she had given up by refusing him. He dropped a bag of silver dollars, like the thirty pieces of silver in the famed story of Judas, at her feet. Mrs. Fletcher told me her grandmother, Eloise, just lowered the basket of laundry to the ground, looked at Stanley and said, "I'll burn in hell before I take one of those silver dollars!" Then she lifted the basket and went home and did other people's laundry.

Eloise Fletcher had a lot in common with the oak trees she planted.

THE BIG BANG THEORY AND A GARDEN RAKE

By the way, I have come to the conclusion that God, like the trees we so desperately wanted to save, has everything to do with shade and nothing to do with power and control. Before I began keeping a journal about the history of punk music, I had chosen a different subject. I started to compile all the big questions and nagging complaints I would ask God when I met him after I died. For instance, why do all the healthy foods like Brussels sprouts, which of course are really good for the body, lack the taste, say, of a charbroiled triple-stacked burger and a super-sized serving of fries? I was taught in catechism class that (A) God loves all of us and (B) God has absolute power and control. So, the way I looked at it as I wrote my journal entry, God had two choices: Either make every vegetable taste like a triple-stacker or make that triple-stacker as healthy as a glass of V8 tomato juice. That's what I wanted to ask God. Why did all unhealthy food taste so darn good?

I also suggested in my journal that there should be a gift store in heaven. Then people who have made it to heaven could buy postcards in the gift shop and send them to their living loved ones. The familiar comment, "Wish you were here," when printed on a postcard sent from heaven, would certainly take on a whole new shine. I also thought the angels should record a Christmas album of all the popular carols and sell it in the gift shop. Heaven knows—everybody else has cashed in on the holiday spirit.

While writing about all of this, I held the mistaken idea that God was a power-hungry control freak. I was wrong.

I came to this updated idea of God many years later on the day I shopped at what was called "the Big Bang Sale" at the local hardware store. I needed to buy a garden rake. It was the very last day of the sale, and it was also the last day of business for Mr. Raymond, the owner of the hardware store. A big mega chain store had opened and priced his small store out of business. I talked with Mr. Raymond for some time and listened to his sad story. In the end, he told me to take the garden rake for free. He told everyone in the store that in ten minutes, he would close his shop forever, so they could take whatever they wanted for free.

Well, there was an explosion of activity as people grabbed at the remains of the store's carcass and carried the bones out the door, which wasn't even one of those automatic doors that opened whenever a customer walked in or out, like in the big mega chain stores. I stood there with my garden rake and looked into the eyes of a good man who had just allowed everything to go out his door. I think it's the same with God—the beginning of our universe, the big bang, was just a cosmic event hosted by a decent guy who didn't feel the need to hear the cosmic cash register ring one more time.

Everything, indeed, had to go.

I felt bad for Mr. Raymond. He had run a decent business, the backbone of America, for thirty-three years. He gave me a garden rake for nothing at all. "This is really sad," I told him.

"Why?" he asked.

"You're going out of business."

"Sure," he said, "but I beat them."

"How?"

"That rake," he said. "Is it cheaper over there?" He pointed in the direction of the mega chain store.

"It was free," I said. "You gave it to me for free."

"That's right. They say they won't be undersold." He laughed in a sad, resigned way. His laughed reminded me of old Otis' laugh. "Well, I undersold them," he said. "I beat those bastards! Take that rake over there and demand some cash. They won't be undersold. That's what they say. My rake was free. Demand a couple of bucks rebate because their rake was more expensive than mine."

I guess he was right. He had undersold the big mega chain store. That's a really difficult thing for a small-business owner to do. I started to walk out the door, but I stood for a moment. I wanted to say something, ask some question, hug the guy, and give him some money. I just wanted to do something.

There was a store just across the street. It was Rob's Grocery Store. It's really strange, but this was really Rob's store. There was a guy called Rob in the small store. He was flesh and blood and often thanked customers for shopping. So I walked across the street and bought a gallon of ice cream. I bought the local stuff, Cedar Crest, and I like to think it's as good as anything else in the universe. I once suggested to Henry Thumm that aliens came to our planet for that ice cream. Henry just nodded in agreement as he ate another scoop.

I found Mr. Raymond as he was unlocking his car door.

"Here," I said. "This is for you. Do you like ice cream?"

There were tears in the old man's eyes, but my ice cream had nothing to do with those tears.

"Thanks," he said.

"It's for the garden rake. It's the least I could do."

His tears persisted. Then he said, "I'm crying."

"I know."

"I'm crying because I owned that hardware store for thirty-three years. My life is over now."

"You'll get another job," I said.

"Sure," he said. "I'll have to get another job. But that's not it."

He paused and had to wipe away a tear. "It's just that when I was young, I didn't want to do anything but own a hardware store. I was lucky. Other kids didn't know what they wanted out of life. But I knew. I thought selling stuff—you know, shovels, and hoes, and rakes for the garden—was the greatest thing a man could do.

"I thought my little store could make people happy.

"They bought stuff to grow things in their garden. I was part of all the gardens in this area. When someone grew tomatoes, or when someone else grew beans or carrots, I grew tomatoes, beans, and carrots, too. I liked to think they were looking forward to talking and planning with me. I liked to think they enjoyed my little store. That was, for some reason, important to me.

"That's the reason I came to work every day. I enjoyed every day. That's what I was thinking when I hired employees. I wanted them to enjoy every day, too."

I suddenly realized his little store had a life of its own. I realized Mr. Raymond was a benign Dr. Frankenstein, and his shop selling garden rakes was a beautiful creation that was now, sadly, to be left vacant and marked with a For Sale sign. That benign creation had realized there was no love for it in our mega chain store world and had simply committed suicide.

"I was wrong," he said slowly.

I noticed the ice cream had begun to melt, but it didn't matter.

"I was wrong because I thought all the people came into my store because they loved to garden. I thought they came into my store because they liked to talk about gardening. But I was wrong."

"How?" I asked.

"They only cared about money. They just wanted to plant money and grow more of it. I was just another store." He paused.

THE BIG BANG THEORY AND A GARDEN RAKE

"But then they were cheaper." He pointed in the direction of the mega chain store.

"I'm sorry," I said.

"A garden shouldn't do that."

"Do what?" I asked.

"Grow money. Care about money. Sell money. I wasn't in business for that. I just wanted to help people tend their gardens."

I suppose the old man was right, but I couldn't find any words to trump his wisdom. So I was silent.

"Oh. I don't really think anybody will miss this old store," he said. "So don't be sorry. You should feel sorry for the people who will buy a garden rake from someone who only wants a paycheck and doesn't care about the dirt and the seeds. You should feel sorry for someone who buys a garden rake from someone who doesn't know the shape and size of every garden in the city."

I realized this man who owned a hardware store had somehow acquired a Ph.D. without ever contemplating an undergraduate degree. This man knew all about our dirt, and he knew how to coax beauty from our soil—which is the greatest thing anyone can ever do. He knew all about decay and death. Old Mr. Raymond knew more about Shakespeare's *Hamlet* and bungholes than all the smart people who study that literary stuff all the time. All I could do was offer him ice cream that was sadly melting—like soft and beautifully tragic Wisconsin dairy land tears.

"Thanks," he said.

"Enjoy your garden rake. It's made in America, you know. Check the label. Everything in my store was made in America. I always made certain of that. My store employed people in Ohio, or Michigan, or whatever state cared to make good stuff."

I said, "Good luck."

He said, "Call me Charlie."

So I called him Charlie. I said, "You're Charlie—the guy who gave me such a beautiful garden rake."

We were, perhaps in some weird way, knights of a real round table.

I decided Mr. Raymond's face should be added to the faces on Mount Rushmore. His face should be on one of our coins or postal stamps.

The ice cream, I'm sure, continued to melt as I sadly walked away from that hardware store.

I was about to begin another journal entry that would speculate on the retail price of various planets, or possibly the actual value of our Milky Way Galaxy, but I was interrupted. Mrs. Fletcher's nephew, Franklin, showed his sorry face. He arrived in a city hall vehicle driven by Thomas Goast, the chief city engineer and chief city everything. This man exuded the power of politics in the way he walked and talked. He had the power of politics even in the way he played poker. He knew the cards were always in his favor. Money talks. Money gets its way. Money is always dealt better cards. Money can always avoid the draft. Money can buy a fifth ace.

"So, how are my trees?" Franklin asked.

"They aren't your trees yet."

"How's the old boy?" He looked at Otis.

"The old boy is just fine."

Thomas Goast leaned against a tree. "Which one's Noah?" he asked.

"That one," I said, as I pointed my finger.

"Well," he said to Noah, "we're going to make you into an ark."

THE BIG BANG THEORY AND A GARDEN RAKE

They both laughed. I couldn't even make a sarcastic comment in reply. That was an odd feeling.

"Which one is the old woman?" Thomas asked.

"You mean Eloise?"

"Yeah. The old lady."

I pointed to the tree next to Noah.

Franklin gave her a shove. "I think this old woman is about ready to fall."

Old Otis growled.

Thomas Goast looked at all the trees. "Which one," he asked, "which one died of the plague?"

I thought about Erna and her stuffed dog. I thought about Erna and her laugh. "She's the one," I said, "she's the one you're leaning against. "He jumped away from the tree. He jumped. Otis barked. I swear the oak tree swayed in an air that had no wind at all.

"She's not contagious, is she?" he asked with a fear that Otis enjoyed. He barked again.

"Tell that stupid dog to shut up," Franklin said. "It's only a matter of time. I know my aunt loved that basset, but it's only a matter of time. I know about the will. When that dog dies, well, all of these trees are gone. They are pulp! They are cardboard boxes and toilet paper! Understand? These trees will be signs telling everybody about the apartments for rent! They are down! You know what I mean? They are down!"

I suddenly saw Vietnam in his eyes. It was such a wasted vision, a vision of the television news with soldiers who hated being soldiers, and I saw a Huey helicopter, and I saw images of wounded soldiers. I saw their blood that still stains television screens so they look like dirty fishbowls for sale at flea markets, even after all these years.

THE GOSPEL ACCORDING TO DARA

I saw Vietnam in his eyes—bloody fishbowls—like bloody memories in a confessional. That's all that was left. There was just Vietnam in his eyes. There was the spittle of fear and a few bloody tears. Then—Poof! There was no fear. There were no tears. Everything was gone. The television had been turned off.

We both looked at these old oaks. There was no compromise. I should have cursed, but I could not find the bullet in my throat. So I didn't curse. I simply understood Franklin. For a moment I understood his hatred for those old trees. They were a jungle. They were the causeway to his past. They were evil. They were wounded friends. They were the dead who ceased to cry in hope of morphine. They were the morphine he hated because it never arrived fast enough to help his friends. The morphine never cried. Franklin didn't see the lovely old oak trees. They were just foliage. He just saw morphine that never arrived in time to stop the cries of pain. They were just Vietnam and tears and blood and vegetation.

It was, indeed, a sad reality to comprehend poor Franklin. I apologized to the world. I think that I laughed. Then I apologized again. Who was I to laugh? Who was I to apologize? Perhaps the universe is simply too big to accept an apology.

Thomas Goast, the big city official who had spent years and years in college instead of going to war in Vietnam, watched Franklin closely. Thomas knew he was the face of city hall. Thomas Goast knew he wanted this area converted into revenue and tax dollars. He assumed a polite façade and tried to be nice.

"Never mind us," Thomas Goast said. "We're just snooping around." He smiled a city hall smile. "By the way," he asked, "which one was the fighter pilot?"

I pointed to Paul. I remembered the old photo of a young Paul showing him alive, quite happy, and a member of the Lafayette

THE BIG BANG THEORY AND A GARDEN RAKE

Escadrille. That photo had been taken the day before he died. He smiled in that picture.

"He's a hero," Thomas said. His voice suddenly had an emotive quaver to it. It was his city hall voice. "You know. When we do this..." His voice trailed off.

"This?" I asked.

"Yeah, you know. When we develop this area."

"You mean when you cut down all the trees?"

"Well, sure. Cut trees. Plant trees. It's all about the same thing." He paused. "But if you let me finish," his voice became emotional again, "when we're all done here, we can, you know, put up a plaque to the guy." He thought for a moment. "Paul. That was his name, wasn't it? We'll put up a plaque. He deserves it. He was a hero. He died for America, and America is all about what we will do here. Build things. Make money. I think Paul would be proud of all of us."

I stood there silently and waited for the guy to sing "The Star-Spangled Banner" or something from the Betsy Ross songbook. Finally, I just said, "And I suppose George Washington cut that cherry tree down to make room for a new high-rise slave quarters."

Thomas Goast lost his polite façade and just said, "Great men cut down great trees."

Franklin had returned from his Vietnam memory. "The way it is," he suddenly interjected, "is these trees have about the same life expectancy as that old dog." He pointed right at Otis.

I looked at Otis.

Otis looked at me.

I think we both gulped. Then I said, "Otis is like a cat. He's got at least nine lives. Watch this!" I spoke with some sort of authority. I picked up Otis' ball and threw it some distance. "Go on, Otis," I ordered. "Fetch it up! Bring me the ball! Show them your stuff. Show them! Get the ball!"

Unfortunately, the old dog just looked at me like I was crazy. Thomas Goast laughed a city hall laugh.

"Come on, old boy!" I pleaded. "Get the ball! Show them!" I was still crazy.

It was time for a serious heart-to-heart talk. I huddled next to Otis. I brushed those two long strands of hair on the top of his head. Perhaps they were lucky.

"This is important," I whispered. "These are evil people, and they want to cut all the trees down. Remember? I showed you those pictures of girl dogs. Now you have to get that ball. Show them. All right?" I pleaded with him. "Show them how long they are going to have to wait." I was hardly confident, but I threw the ball anyway.

"Get it, Otis!" I shouted.

Otis just sighed.

I thought about that tree, Eloise. I thought about the silver dollars Stanley had thrown at her feet. Stanley. Stanley Goast. Thomas. Thomas Goast. They had to be related—related like the tombstone bearing their family name, related through privilege, related through power, related through money, related through vengeance.

"Otis!" I pleaded again. This ballgame was no longer about the batter at the plate. It wasn't about just getting out of the inning and leaving a few runners on the bases. No, this ballgame was about this season, last season—next season—every season. It was about every pitch and every batter and every stolen base and every third-base coach waving the runner home. It was about playing center field. "Come on, Otis!" I pleaded with the old dog. "Be a Brewer! Be Robin Yount!" I thought about the stars of the major league. "Be Gorman Thomas! Yeah! Be Stormin' Gorman! Be Paul Molitor!"

The sad basset eyes just sagged in response.

I was reaching for anything. I was reaching for the moon. "Be Hank Aaron! Be Hammerin' Hank!" I yelled. Hank Aaron had returned to Milwaukee at the very end of his career. Sure, the Braves had moved to Atlanta, but that didn't matter. I just wanted Otis to chase the ball.

Franklin tossed his cigarette butt to the ground, and it bounced off Erna's bark before it smoldered in her dirt. So I just cried out, "Otis! Be Babe Ruth! You know! Be Babe Ruth!"

Well, to my surprise, that old basset's heart suddenly beat with the fires of youth. I swear! Those old basset ears perked up. Those basset eyes were large and round like the very coins Eloise had rejected. That old dog ran with all the gusto of a rookie base runner rounding third and heading for home! Hallelujah! Hallelujah! Hallelujah! Otis snagged that ball on its very first bounce. Hallelujah again!

Old Otis returned the ball and was, indeed, ready for more action. His grab reminded me of Willy Mays and his famous over-the-shoulder catch. It was a work of art. So I yelled, "Be Willy Mays!" Otis' tail stopped wagging.

I had to think quickly.

I told him, "All right! Be Pete Rose!" He danced on the very spot on which he stood. His short legs seemed reluctant even to touch the ground.

I tossed the ball. This time, it didn't even manage a first bounce. I was stunned with delight. Mister Hustle, indeed!

Thomas Goast and Franklin looked worried.

Otis returned the ball. His muzzle grinned. Those two old strands of white-tipped hair were raised with defiance. Don't

70

tread on me! Don't shoot until you see the whites of their eyes! Nuts! I shall return! And, by the way, don't cut down these lovely old trees! God save those trees!

Thomas Goast swore. It was a city hall curse word. Franklin was off into another Vietnam memory. This old dog, whose death was so crucial to their plans, had suddenly shown an intense spark of life. This, most certainly, was a big problem for them. They wanted to cut down all the trees and build some big apartment complex, where they could shove a person into a tiny space that looked just like another tiny space into which they could shove some other person. Their plan was all about money.

Otis dropped the ball and growled at them. The old boy really let them have it.

Franklin tried to redeem the situation.

"When we were in Vietnam," he said, "we never had to ask any of these questions or get anyone's permission. We never had to wait. If we wanted a parking lot, we just flattened everything and made that parking lot."

"Where would you put it?" Thomas Goast asked.

"Right over there." Franklin pointed at the trees that bore Peter and Daniel's names.

Otis growled again.

Franklin tore off a piece of Eloise's bark. "We'll give them a garage. You know, these people care more about their precious cars than anything else. We can charge them more."

Otis growled a third time.

"Good boy!" I said.

"You just keep your chubby little growls to yourself," Thomas Goast said. "You don't have too many left. I wouldn't waste any more on us." They slowly walked back to their city hall vehicle and slammed their city hall doors. I put my arm around Otis.

THE BIG BANG THEORY AND A GARDEN RAKE

He was panting from all the excitement. Even his rebellious hair sprouts seemed to droop because they were tired.

"Otis," I said, as I attempted to prop up those two white hairs, "you still need that haircut. And," I added, "if I have any say in the matter, that's the way it's always going to be."

That was, oddly enough, a comment lacking my usual sarcasm: I think it was a good thing to say. After all these years, I think that it was an extremely important thing to say.

I was never going to cut those hairs—those lovely outlaws of the follicle world.

Between

LYDIA MAENAD SAT NEXT TO ME. For some reason, I always thought of her as Lydia when she was angry with me. She was just Liddy when I managed to keep my mouth shut.

She was reading my notebook, reading my "History of Punk Music." That was the title on the very top of the notebook page. I watched as she read everything I had written. "It's just a rough draft," I said. I was a little embarrassed to have her read my ideas. I never allowed anyone to read what I wrote.

Liddy raised one finger. Then she said, "Sweet momento."

I knew her too well. She only said that silly phrase when she was seriously interested and needed to concentrate. She was asking me to give her a moment to think. I watched as her long beautiful blond dreadlocks brushed against the pages of my notebook. This was my notebook, and that was her hair. She seemed interested. Sweet momento, indeed! Her finger remained silently in the air. Finally, she blinked. Then she asked, "Who's this Haydn guy with the wig music?"

"Well," I explained, "he was a classical composer. His *Surprise Symphony* blew the wigs off the rich women who came to hear his new music while being seen in high society."

"Did he want to blow their wigs off?"

BETWEEN

"I think so."

She thought for a moment. "All right. Yeah. I see your point. So he wrote that music to blow those rich wigs right off?"

"Sure," I said. "It probably rattled their fancy jewelry, too."

She raised that finger again. She paused. "You know you should include Phil Ochs in here."

"Phil Ochs?"

"Yeah. He's protest. He's punk. Yeah. He was just really angry with America." She thought for a moment. Then she added, "But I think he loved America, too."

"Why?"

"Because he wanted to tell the truth about Vietnam and Nixon," she said. "Listen to his song 'Crucifixion' or 'Another Age.' They're as good as The Sex Pistols or The Clash."

"Really?"

"Yeah," she explained. "Punk is just an attitude. Bob Marley is punk. He matters. Listen to 'Redemption Song.' It's all about the same thing. The Beatles were punk when they began. They wanted to be punk at the end. That's the way it should be."

I thought about those two white strains of hair on the top of Otis' head that refused to comply with society's demands. I loved those white tufts of hair. In an odd way, they were all part of this. They were punk. So I decided to write about that tuft. Otis needed a haircut. That line just occurred to me as I sat next to Liddy. Much later, of course, I would use the sentence as the beginning of this story. Serendipity may well be the order of the universe.

Liddy was still talking.

"You haven't talked about Doll by Doll or Wire. Where's Roy Harper? What about Patti Smith? What about The Cure? Robert Smith just screams all the time. 'All Cats Are Grey.' Do you know that one? How about 'The Holy Hour'? That's all he wants to do. He just wants to scream. He's no different from Joy Division or Magazine or The Ramones. And Dylan. What about Dylan? He should be in here. You have to put Dylan in here."

"It's not a novel," I said. "It's just a few journal pages I've got to write because my psychiatrist said I have a problem with anger."

Boy, was I wrong.

"You don't have a problem with anger. You never get mad. I get mad all the time. But you," she paused, "you only have a problem with anger because you never get mad."

"Well," I said. "That's one way of looking at it."

I leaned forward and tickled Otis' ears. He rested on the ground in front of us. "And I'm sorry," I finally said. "I'm sorry about making fun of your sign. Dr. Rein said I'm supposed to stop that sort of stuff, too."

"Sarcasm?" she asked.

"Yeah. And you don't have to ritualistically shave your head."

"How about skipping backward?" she asked.

"Yeah," I added. "And you don't have to sing Captain and Tennille songs either."

She smiled and asked," Why do those albums always end up in thrift stores?"

"I don't know. But one day I want to ask the thrift-shop people if I could categorize their albums like real record stores do."

"What do you mean?"

"Well," I suggested, "all the records that are always there will have their own section, like the Captain and Tennille. Those Herb Alpert whipped-cream albums, you know, he would have his own section with a label that reads 'Herb Alpert and the Tijuana Brass.' All of those albums with the woman covered in whipping cream on the cover. They're always there. That way, if

I wanted his music, I would know where to look, just like in a real record store.

"Sometimes," I said, "I believe that's why God put me on Earth. Some people run really fast. Some people find great cures for terrible diseases. Some people invent stuff. Maybe God decided one day he needed someone to organize the records in thrift shops. It wouldn't do much for humanity, but it might help out a couple of people looking for a good deal on used vinyl."

She laughed, and then said, "There would have to be a section for the Osmonds. Donny could have his own solo spot."

"Would you," I asked, "put the *Saturday Night Fever* soundtrack under John Travolta or the Bee Gees?"

"That's a tough question." She looked intentionally sincere. "I think," she said. "There are enough copies in most of those stores to spread the guilt. Put a few in both spots."

So we both agreed to do this someday. It would revolutionize thrift-store record buying. No more stacks and stacks of bad Christmas albums. They would be conveniently stuffed into the section labeled just that—"Bad Christmas Albums." This would follow the section labeled "Bad Accordion Albums" but would precede "Bad Inspirational Albums."

Question: What do Don Ho, Jim Nabors, Kenny Rogers, and just about everybody in the universe have in common?

Answer: Bad Inspirational Albums.

My Liddy was back. She was dressed in her usual dark-colored dress, non-matching tights, and high-topped tennis shoes. Today her dress was a deep red and her tights were blue. This was the woman Mrs. Fletcher told me to marry. Of course, Mrs. Fletcher was quite dead when she made the suggestion, so I wasn't certain it counted for anything.

"And The Rezillos and The Buzzcocks. And Kevin Coyne.

THE GOSPEL ACCORDING TO DARA

And Ian Hunter," she suddenly said. "They all have that attitude. You have to include them in your journal." She could have gone on forever. I really didn't care anymore. I just loved that deep red dress, those blue tights, high-topped tennis shoes, and blond dreadlocks still resting on the pages of my notebook. "Eddie and the Hot Rods," she said. "And Siouxsie Sue." Liddy went on and on like a great sale of used vinyl that far exceeds the patience of the most loving wife waiting in the car.

Of course, she could go on and on. I was just happy that she was sitting next to me. I was fascinated. She had given her soul to all this music—music that made her angry and excited. I liked music, but all I could ever do was write a song like "White Gold," which was about smuggling illegal oleomargarine across state lines. I used music to make fun of the stupidity I saw all around me. I used music to survive in the world of stupidity. Liddy, on the other hand, used music to impale her passions on the wall of injustice and tragedy. Music allowed her to kick at all the darkness in the world—a kick with those lovely high-topped sneakers.

Otis rolled over. That was his response to the world. I leaned over and tickled his big round belly. That was my response to the world. Mrs. Fletcher had given him too many treats. I stopped for a second. He barked because he wanted more tickling, so I complied. I didn't want him to waste any more barks. He should save them for Thomas Goast and Franklin Fletcher.

Then Liddy suddenly asked, "Joshua, do you ever get mad about, you know, not ever getting mad?"

"Is that possible?" I asked.

"What do you mean?"

"Well," I just couldn't resist the opportunity, "in math class, what did they say? If a negative number is subtracted from another negative number, don't they suddenly become positive?"

"Could be," she said. "I never could figure any of that stuff out."

"I'm sure it's a positive number."

"So?"

Who was I to resist temptation? Eve just offered up yet another apple. Adam will always be Adam, and an apple will always be an apple. It may look like a burrito or a triple-stacked hamburger, but it's still an apple. So I just said, "Well, what's a positive number? I mean, is it a positive thing to get angry? Or is it a positive thing not to get mad?"

Liddy's eyes turned pizza-oven hot. Lydia was back, and she was angry. "You just make a joke out of everything." She was mad. "It was a question, and I meant something serious. All you can do is joke."

For some reason I thought about Adam. Perhaps he took the apple just to be sarcastic. Perhaps he thought, at least in his version of the story, God had a much better sense of humor about his supply of fresh produce. "I'm sorry," I said.

Guys always say that. I'm sure if God had been married, he also would have said he was sorry.

"Josh," she said, "I was just trying to talk to you. I thought you could do something more than scratch a dog's belly." She seldom called me Josh.

To be completely honest, I wasn't sure men could really evolve any further than that—the ability to scratch a dog's belly—which, I suppose, is an evolutionary quantum leap from scratching his own belly. But I kept my mouth shut. I am eternally grateful I managed to keep my mouth shut at that moment.

"I don't know," she said. "It's easy to get angry. I mean Ronald Reagan is about to be elected President of the United States.

Aren't we all ashamed? Think about it. Ronald Reagan. Ronald Reagan. President of our United States! The guy is just an old actor. And all you can do is make a joke! If you have seen one redwood, you've seen them all. That's what Reagan said! Trees cause more pollution than cars. That's what he said! All you can do is joke!" She was on a Lydia roll. Boy, could she get mad! "Then the students in California protested. All he could say was let the bloodbath begin! I thought the British did that sort of thing in Boston. I thought we hated them for it. The Boston Massacre! How about the Berkeley Massacre? How about Kent State? Should we shoot protesters again? Aren't you ashamed?"

She was livid. She was Lydia.

I said again that I was sorry. Guys do that a lot. Even sarcastic guys do that a lot.

Then we find a dog's belly to scratch.

More
of the
Big Bang Theory
and a bit of
Dog Latin

BAD NEWS: OTIS DIED.

Let's see, Lydia was still sitting next to me, and, of course, she was still angry. She was always angry, so there was silence between us. What could I say? Nothing. That's why there was just a silence between us.

I looked at Otis. I was so proud of the old boy. He chased anything as long as I mentioned Pete Rose and Babe Ruth. That wasn't a difficult thing to figure out.

You see, Jenny Egolenski, the poet who wrote all the song lyrics for Reagan Rally, or whatever they chose to call themselves, owned a dog named Dara, and Dara's full name was Dara Ruthie Rose. Leave it to Jenny to give a dog a long important name. I knew why old Otis chased that ball. It was because I had mentioned the words, Ruth and Rose. In those words, he heard the name of his true love—Jenny Egolenski's Irish setter, Dara Ruthie Rose. It is, indeed, a small world.

So I had it all figured out: Old Otis chased that ball because of pride. He chased it out of pure stamina. He chased it out of love. Guys do that sort of thing all the time. Why should male dogs be any different?

Yes, I had it all figured out.

MORE OF THE BIG BANG THEORY
AND A BIT OF DOG LATIN

Otis loved Dara.

Lydia continued to read my journal. She was waiting for Belle to pick her up. They were going to Spooky's—a costume shop on Green Bay's west side. It was an odd place to go in August because the place made most of its money during the Halloween season.

She suddenly asked, "What's this first part?"

I glanced at the page. "That's the other topic. When I get tired with the history of punk music, I write about that one."

"What is it?"

"Well," I said, trying to explain my metaphysical persona. "Those are more questions I'm going to ask God when I die and get to talk to him. I mean, so far, they are mostly gripes, but I suppose I'll find something he did well."

God isn't concerned with power and control. We humans want that stuff. God simply gave everything away at the beginning of the universe. That's why the meaning of life is so incomprehensible to us.

We humans are always barking up the wrong tree, so to speak, and griping to God a lot about bad luck. The way I figure it that would be like blaming good old Mr. Raymond if I strained a muscle while weeding my garden with the rake he gave me.

Anyway, as I was sitting next to Liddy while she was reading the journal Dr. Rein had asked me to write, I still held the customary belief God was the ultimate source of power and control in the universe.

Liddy looked up from my journal with an excited smile. She liked reading my deep and private thoughts about life, and I watched eagerly as she read my ideas.

"So," she said with a stunned expression. She looked right at me and sort of yelled, "You mean to tell me that the first thing you would ask God is whether he liked ice cream?"

"My questions are not necessarily in any order. They're just ideas." I paused. "But sure. All he probably hears is praying and complaining, so this might give him the chance to talk about himself for a change. It's just an icebreaker. It works when guys are out with women. Women like to talk about themselves."

"Joshua," she deepened her voice, "and how many times has Mr. Icebreaker actually talked with a woman in his life?"

"Does my mother count?"

She didn't answer me.

"Does my sister count? How about you, Liddy?" I said. "You're a woman. You count, don't you?"

"Yes, I count. And I don't need a calculator to know the answer. It's zero. Zero dates." She read a little bit more. Then she suddenly looked up. "What if God says 'yes'?'"

"'Yes' about what?"

"'Yes' because he means 'yes.' 'Yes' because he likes ice cream."

"Then we talk flavors."

"And what if God doesn't like ice cream?"

"Then I guess we rule out dairy products as a whole." I added, "But we could still talk about oleomargarine because, as you know, it's a well-known butter substitute. It's not a dairy product, per se."

She laughed and again pointed to my journal. "What's this Italy idea?"

MORE OF THE BIG BANG THEORY
AND A BIT OF DOG LATIN

"I haven't figured it out yet," I confessed. "But I just thought if God spent so much time and effort into making Italy look like a boot, then why wasn't he a bit more clever and creative with some other countries?"

She thought about various countries and then said, "I don't think God could have done much with Canada."

"Sure, Canada's a tough one. It's Canada. It's just there. But think about Japan or Iceland. Think about Cuba."

"All right. That's not too bad. It's better than the ice cream question." She continued reading and then asked, "So, you think that God should have arranged it so we would all know the exact day of our death a few days beforehand?"

"Well," I offered, "then there would be no surprises."

"Maybe surprises are a good thing." She thought for a moment. "I like presents."

Quite frankly, I had never thought of death as a present, although a band called Mott the Hoople that I had referenced in my history of punk music journal wrote a song called "Death May Be Your Santa Claus." They took the title from a band called Secondhand, who stole the title from a movie of the same name. That noted, I still had never thought of death as a gift; however, I managed to keep my mouth shut.

Liddy smiled and said, "I think I understand. But I still like surprises."

"Well," I said, "remember, it's just an idea. I had to write something, so I wrote that. I was just filling time and space."

Then she just said to me, "Why didn't you write about Debbie?"

I would swear I heard the sound of a hammer cracking time and space.

"Debbie?" I said.

THE GOSPEL ACCORDING TO DARA

My world fell apart again.

"You know, Debbie Finch. Why didn't you write about her in your journal? Why didn't you ask God why she had to die? Why didn't you ask God why nice people die from brain tumors and evil people never seem to have those brain tumors?"

She struck a hot nerve, so I was naked —without Novocain injected into any cell of my body.

"Remember when you told me about Debbie? You told me about Debbie and her tumor, and you told me that God didn't care. Debbie had blue eyes. That's what you said. She had Halloween eyes. That's what you said."

I remembered everything I said. Debbie's eyes were Halloween eyes.

There are spaces between everything—even words. So I filled those spaces with one concrete question: Why did Debbie Finch have to die? Debbie Finch had some sort of brain tumor while we were in the third grade. Everybody else had hair on our heads. We were kids—but Debbie had a big scar instead of hair.

One time Liddy and I were walking out of church. We were with our parents. We were just little kids. Families still went to church together in the family car. God was our friend who answered our prayers. I glanced back at Debbie—another little kid who believed in God. Her family's car was a red Ford station wagon. She stood there with a scarf on her head to cover the scar. She was with her parents, too. Liddy had such beautiful hair. I had regular guy hair, and we were walking into the morning of the rest of our lives.

Debbie had but a few weeks to live.

I glanced back. Debbie looked at me. Her parents looked at her. I couldn't even recall one word of the priest's sermon. I could only avert my eyes to the plastic Jesus as he silently bled on his cross. My mother took my hand in hers as we left the church.

Liddy knew some stuff, but she didn't know some other stuff.

We were in art hour—the bit of time when math and reading were put aside and creativity was the order of the moment. I was drawing a bird. That's what I always did. The teacher made a big deal of this. On that day, she said, "Birds symbolize your imagination in flight, Joshua!" This was a normal thing for a teacher to say.

I remember my response: "I didn't draw a bird. I drew the ghost of a bird."

That was an odd thing for a third-grader to say.

There was this kid—much older, a sixth-grader. He was a friend of Jonathan Maened. His name was Mo Rainbow. He had freckles on his ears. I remember that. Nobody else had freckles on their ears. He would talk to me—which was odd. Once, he took me aside and gave me a serious look."Listen," he said, "if they ever try to get you to look into a microscope, for God's sake, don't do it."

"Why not?" I asked.

He simply said, "You don't wanna know."

"Have you done it?" I asked.

"Yeah," he confessed. "They got me in fifth grade."

"So what did you see?" I asked.

He just said, "Trust me. You don't wanna know."

Another time, he told me he saw ghosts all the time.

So I asked if he saw any famous dead people. I asked him if he saw Abraham Lincoln—who, to my third-grade mind, was a famous dead person.

"No," he said. "I don't get to see that stuff anymore. I've seen ghosts of dogs, ghosts of trees, ghosts of holes in the ground. But Abe Lincoln? He's just dead to me."

In a weird third-grade way, I hoped this ear-freckled kid was wrong. I wanted to see ghosts of people. I hoped he was wrong, and then I figured this had something to do with his fifth-grade glimpse into the microscope's lens. There was so much I "didn't want to know."

I remember the look in Debbie's eyes. Were they truly Halloween eyes? No. They were much darker because they contained no grinning pumpkin to illuminate my three-stall garage—but the teacher came in and told us all, "Debbie has gone to a much better place."

Zorro never really bothered to exist. It was always Debbie. And it will always be the ghost of Debbie.

I simply said, "You have to be much more specific. That could be just about anywhere."

We were in the middle of art class—an oasis in the midst of math and science. I stopped dead in mid–pencil scrawl. I was drawing a bird. I stopped. I never finished that bird, and the teacher never again told me a bird was a flight of my imagination. Debbie was dead. I stopped my drawing. The teacher said, "She has gone to a much better place." I made a sarcastic comment.

But these weren't my words. They were, somehow, Debbie's thoughts.

Years later, I would hear Mrs. Fletcher tell me to marry Liddy. All these words were just about the same. I had to keep saying those words. They were my mantra. They were my koan. Those words were a mysterious Fatima rosary to me.

Everything was fine at that moment. I was sitting next to Liddy. Paradise, indeed, reigned. Belle arrived, hand in hand with Moses. Moses' brother, Elvis, was with them. I had not known the kid was missing part of his left arm. No one said anything, but I just figured the rest of his arm was probably left in Vietnam, due to a child's lack of understanding of the effects of explosives. Were the explosives our explosives or theirs? Did it really matter?

I heard Belle explain some of the tree history to Moses. I heard her mention Paul and Erna. Then she told him about Thecla, who was named after someone who was erased from the Bible. She told him some people believed the names of Eloise and Noah were etched in the heart of each tree.

Belle said something about space alien costumes and the store closing.

"Why do you need the costumes?" I asked.

Belle laughed. "It's just a joke. You know Squeegee, don't you?"

"You mean Roswell Robbie?"

"Yeah, you know he's been playing the tough guy and giving Elvis a hard time. We're going to scare him."

"How?"

"You'll see tonight," Moses said. "You'll be there?"

"Sure," I said. But believe me, I wasn't certain about anything. I didn't know their plan, and I couldn't foresee the consequences. So, of course, like an idiot, I just said "Sure."

THE GOSPEL ACCORDING TO DARA

Allow me to explain. Robert "Squeegee" Reynolds, aka Roswell Robbie, was the goalkeeper who protected all things Caucasian in the universe. I don't believe, even to this day, that he was crazy. It was just that everything "alien" frightened him. For example, he never ate in a Chinese restaurant, and he never even had a burrito from Taco Bell. Robbie worked in the local car wash, and he hated Japanese cars, though I don't think he hated German cars—which was odd. But the kid lived in absolute fear of anything outside the limited sphere of his understanding, and basically Squeegee's understanding was limited to three fixed laws of nature.

To paraphrase his own words, he (1) hated all aliens—illegal, legal, and extraterrestrial, (2) believed people of color should quickly return to colored countries, and (3) believed aliens from other planets were coming to enslave all the white people on Earth, intending to place the white men in forced-labor camps and use the white women as sex slaves. This was no joke to him, and it was also no joke to us. Unfortunately, we didn't realize it at the time. The guy was dead certain that alien creatures in flying saucers would one day descend from the heavens and destroy his family's farmhouse, barn, and his pet dog, affectionately known as Bullet.

Everyone just called him Squeegee because his greatest aim in life was to work at the local car wash. That didn't help the situation. It didn't help that everyone also knew him as "Roswell Robbie" due to his fear of all things alien. The kid lived in constant fear. Perhaps that was the reason he was so mean to Moses' brother Elvis and the other Vietnamese refugees who were relocated to our area.

"War," Moses said as he looked at all the trees. "Death." The guy knew more than we did about those things.

MORE OF THE BIG BANG THEORY
AND A BIT OF DOG LATIN

I glanced at what was left of Elvis' arm.

"What ever happened to Mrs. Fletcher's husband?" Moses asked.

"She never really said much about love," Belle said slowly. "I know she was never married. She was just Mrs. Fletcher to us. She never changed her name. She loved someone, though. She once said he was one of the boys. She said that she did everything for the boys who fought in the war. 'Everything for the boys' is what all of America said. Then she told me some of the boys just didn't come home like they should have."

As they left for the costume shop, Liddy waved at me. That was a nice thing to do. It was a Belle thing to do. Unfortunately, the same city hall vehicle was back. Apparently, Thomas Goast and Franklin needed to return to their intended crime scene.

"We were talking about that plaque," Thomas Goast said. "Franklin thought that other tree was a hero, too."

"You mean Peter," I said.

"Yeah, Peter. Paul. What the heck? We'll put up plaques for Mathew, Mark, Luke, and John if they're here." He laughed. "After we cut them all down, it won't make any difference."

I desperately wanted to say something that would blow the wigs off everyone. I wanted to kick at this monster until the lifeblood of greed and arrogance and stupidity oozed from it. Liddy, for whom battles came easily, could do that. She had those high-topped tennis shoes and could kick anything. But for me, there was no easy enemy. For a moment, I even sympathized with Franklin. I'm sure he found many enemies in the jungle warfare of his existence. He lashed out at the darkness. I just laughed at it. I was the one who had the problem with anger. At least, that was one way of looking at it. So I smiled and held old Otis' ball.

THE GOSPEL ACCORDING TO DARA

Otis watched me closely.

"Be Babe Ruth," I said. I knew exactly what I was doing. I looked at Thomas Goast and Franklin. They would never understand the big-bang give-a-way theory. Their god was a monument to their own arrogance, a mirror to their own fear. Their god would never give anything away, not even a garden rake. Sure. I didn't know all of this at the time, but I do now. I doubt, even after all these years that they pray to anything other than themselves.

I knew exactly what I was doing. "Be Pete Rose," I told Otis.

He barked. It was almost as if he were revving his old engine for one final race.

Then I threw the ball, and I laughed sarcastically. I truly believed there were, indeed, countless balls to be thrown and fetched. I was so wrong, so incredibly wrong. I knew Otis. I yelled, "Get that ball for Dara and for Ruthie and for Rose!"

Otis ran.

I watched him run, and then everything slowed down. At least it is always slowed in my memory. It's always slow, and it's always sad. I thought old Otis laughed as he grabbed the ball in his basset mouth. That's all he wanted. He wanted the ball because he heard the words "Dara" and "Ruth" and "Rose." Such a simple desire! Such a simple old heart! And I swear I heard that simple heart stop.

Mrs. Fletcher told me to listen to the words never spoken and care about the things that didn't happen—like a missing heartbeat and the silence after the final bark.

His old heart stopped, and life flickered like an old silent movie in his eyes. Otis recovered for a moment. Then he sort of died for another moment. The ball bounced and continued to roll.

Otis was disoriented. He bumped into a tree. He bumped

MORE OF THE BIG BANG THEORY
AND A BIT OF DOG LATIN

into a tree having no name, the one Henry Thumm said was just like the altar the Greeks had for the god they did not know.

Then Otis fell and did not get back up.

I think he was frightened. He wasn't worried about God or hell or heaven because dogs don't know anything about that stuff. Dogs don't build monuments to themselves. He was probably just frightened because he so desperately wanted to retrieve that ball, but he just couldn't do it. That old basset body lay against a tree, barely breathing.

He couldn't bark.

I heard the sound he did not make. I swear I heard that sound. I ran to him and cradled him in my arms.

Otis looked at me. He wanted me to make everything all right, but I just couldn't do it for him. That was the last bit of life I saw in his eyes—his desire for me to make everything all right. I once saw a lovely doctor gently hold a cancer patient's hopeful hand. It was something like that.

I wanted Otis to live. But he was silent. I heard this silence. I knew my Otis was dead.

"How's the old boy doing?" I heard a voice say. It was Franklin. I looked up and saw him leaning against Noah.

Thomas Goast picked at Eloise's bark. "Looks like this is the only bark you have left," he said.

I wanted to vomit and laugh at the same time. That is probably the best explanation for the very human need for sarcasm — the Maginot Line between comedy and tragedy: To vomit or not to vomit? To laugh or not to laugh? That just may well be the question.

"Perhaps we should take the old guy. It might be easier for you," Thomas Goast said, attempting to feign city hall kindness.

I'm certain they said many more things about construction

and apartment buildings and rent payments. Their voices probably sounded like the ring of cash registers, like the beginning of that Pink Floyd song about money. I didn't hear them. I took Mrs. Fletcher's advice and listened to the heartbeat that was not there.

Otis was so peaceful.

He still needed that haircut.

I said absolutely nothing, because truthfully, there were no words to express my sadness. There were only words between those words I did not choose to say.

Then, for some ridiculous reason, I sang "White Gold" to my old basset friend. Oddly enough, it sounded like a lullaby. It was a song conjured from my past. It was certainly never meant to be a drug song, because really, who cares about a well-known butter substitute that isn't even illegal anymore? Yes, it was always meant to be a lullaby. I just never, before that moment, had a reason to sing a lullaby, but I wanted to sing one to Otis.

Afterward, I pretended to pick notes from "America," the song Mrs. Fletcher had asked me to learn. I didn't have a guitar, so there was no sound at all. I read somewhere there's no sound on the planet Mercury, and no trees to make a sound as they fall, and, of course, no creatures to hear the sounds that don't exist. There are no creatures to contemplate philosophical ideas about trees or dogs or sounds. So, for just a moment, this was my world, and I saw the vague shadow of a ghost—a ghost laughing on a crisp Halloween night. In that instant, I fell into eternity—an eternity peacefully resting between the very seconds of all our lives.

MORE OF THE BIG BANG THEORY
AND A BIT OF DOG LATIN

Years later, as I carried the garden rake through the aisle of Mr. Raymond's hardware store in the final moment of its existence, I noticed a small sign in the meager plant and flower section. It read: *Sic transit glories mundi*. Nobody bothered with it, I suppose, because it was in Latin, and who needs a sign written in Latin? I held the sign in my hand.

"Do you know what it says?" he asked.

I didn't have a clue.

"It says," he translated, "thus passes away the glory of the world."

"Kind of like all the years you've owned this store?" I suggested.

He smiled slowly. That's all he managed to do, just smile. As I held that sign in his store, I thought of old Otis. If I had known the phrase at the time he died, I might have repeated that bit of Latin. Those beautiful words need to be whispered as doors are closed, daily, on the uncertain footsteps of our lives.

Extraterrestrial Gothic

BELLE AND LIDDY SAID THEIR PRANK would help me get over Otis' death because pranks make people laugh.

Odd. I never needed help laughing.

But they said everyone would get the joke about aliens and Squeegee. They said everything would be just like a Halloween party. It would be just like bobbing for apples. The snake probably said the same thing to Eve. It's all a party game. That's what they said, but they were wrong.

They were dead wrong.

It was Belle's idea. Naturally, she talked all of us into it. Moses was upset because his Vietnamese relatives simply wanted to be free—just like every other refugee in every other chapter of an American history textbook. My grandfather, for example, had sought refuge in America when he fled Poland in 1915, during World War I.

Some of the Vietnamese had been on our side. I suppose they expected us to know that bit of history. It really wasn't much different here than it was there. It was supposed to be different. That's what we thought. That was the promise.

Belle showed me the silver alien suits she had rented from Spooky's Costume Shop. They were skintight, with large bulbous heads, and the fingers extended with suction cups at the tips. She was given a really good deal because it wasn't Halloween. She was so excited when she showed them to me.

The idea was so simple. Belle and Moses were to wear the silver suits and walk across Squeegee Roswell Robbie Reynolds' yard and give him a close encounter of the up-close-and-hand-shaking-howdy kind.

Moses tried on a glove. He had to practice his handshake, given that his fingers were really elongated with suction-cupped tips. Believe me, it's not an easy thing to do. But the *coup de grace* of the close encounter—which, of course, had Belle's personality written all over it—was to occur when Moses and Belle would pose with a pitchfork held in Moses' silver fingers, in the everyday, every-way, all-time *American Gothic* pose. Belle would hand Squeegee Roswell Robbie a camera and politely ask him to take their picture. Then, the two would thank Squeegee, ask for the camera back, and walk away into a silver-space-suited all-American sunset.

As I said, the plan was so simple.

It is important to note that Moses didn't merely follow Belle into all of this; he was in cahoots from the get-go. His dark serious eyes were the perfect complement for Belle's lighthearted laugh. Ultimately, they were merely two humans who enjoyed each other's presence enough to hold hands most of the time.

So, it was all going to be a joke. I suppose that the *American Gothic* silver-space-suited alien farmer part was some sort of statement about immigrants and America and whatever. But really, it was just a joke—just a joke that went so terribly wrong.

The problem was all of this alien stuff was really no joke to Squeegee Roswell Robbie Reynolds. Sure, he played the clown, but he really was obsessed with alien creatures of any kind. The

THE GOSPEL ACCORDING TO DARA

kid apparently lived in constant fear. That's why he was so nasty to all the Vietnamese people who suddenly made their presence known in our area after the collapse of South Vietnam. Some of those Vietnamese people, if I recall correctly, were clutching the landing gear of our departing helicopters. We watched them on our television screens and cheered for them in a sad sort of way. We all wanted to sweep Vietnam under the rug—a rug that already covered so many Indian wars and too many slave auctions.

Squeegee Roswell Robbie knew enough to hide his fear. Though he didn't know much else, he knew enough to camouflage his weakness. We were unaware that he spent many sleepless nights cradling an army surplus fully loaded semiautomatic rifle while cursing and staring at the evening sky. His parents knew about the gun but thought it was a hobby. They did not know he had filed the safety down to an inconsequential nub.

I kept my usual sarcastic distance from the whole thing. I watched as Moses straightened Belle's silver antennae with his long suction-tipped fingers, and I watched as he grabbed the *American Gothic* pitchfork. I watched, too, as Belle checked the flash in the camera, and I watched as they both walked into the saddest sunset I have ever seen.

Everybody was laughing as Squeegee came out of the house. Of course, he was home alone. It was Thursday night, and his parents were bowling and drinking at the local alley, a weekly ritual for them. We all laughed a bit more because we figured Squeegee was scared.

Someone said something about him deserving all of this.

We laughed as Moses and Belle paused and planted their silver-suited selves in an all-*American Gothic* pose. We continued to chuckle even after the first bullets lit the evening air with their ungodly tracer fire.

The bullets burned on the breeze.

I was close enough to smell the tiny bits of *Dante's Inferno* flaring through the night air—a night air that sagged like hot thick sewage. One bullet hit the wooden handle of the pitchfork and set the damn thing on fire. I am ashamed to say I was still laughing as the first bullet hit Belle. Bullets travel faster than the brain's impulse not to laugh. God should have thought about that. It's a question I need to ask him when I die.

Belle's beautiful legs didn't even buckle. They didn't even have the chance to bend. Bone and skin and vein and silver space suit just exploded into hot spittle that suddenly covered the cool evening grass. The bright harvest moon illuminated the torn wreckage of Belle's bloody legs. I swear to this day, at the moment of impact, Belle's long spidery suction-tipped fingers were intertwined with the suction fingers of Moses' silver alien hands.

You know, we never did know his real name. He was just Moses to all of us: Moses, the prophet from the Bible; Moses, the refugee from Vietnam; Moses, the vocalist from a silly rock band; Moses, the guy who always held hands with Liddy's older sister, Belle; Moses, the dead guy.

The first bullet that struck him blew a big hole through the chest of his silver alien space suit. It was like the pull tab of a big Coke can popping open. The second bullet shot his head off. I remember it all in slow motion, like the Zapruder film of John F. Kennedy's assassination, except Moses never grabbed at his throat like President Kennedy did.

This wasn't Dallas, Texas. This was America after the Vietnam War. This was an America that had seen too much of this sort of violence. This was an America that sent its kids to fight and die for some strange country's freedom and sent its helicopters so Vietnamese people could grab hold and hang on long enough to find a tiny bit of safety and perhaps even some freedom in a world that seldom gave a rat's rectum for such ideas.

I saw Moses' blood, no different in color from the blood that leaked from Belle's wound, blood that came here to be free of the bloodshed in his old country. Belle tried to crawl, but the slippery grass prevented much movement. She was just a heap of screaming silver flesh. Moses didn't move at all.

I thought Liddy would start to yell, but she didn't yell. She just fell on her knees next to Belle, who screamed in a voice that was no longer human. Liddy looked like she was praying, but I really didn't know what she was doing. What would be the point of a prayer? A miracle? There were no miracles that night. So, I just stood and watched as Liddy knelt in the nascent darkness of the descending night—a night dipped in blood, a nascent darkness that lacked any salvation, a nascent darkness that was simply an eternity begging for a finish line.

I saw deep stains on Liddy's high-topped sneakers. Her shoes were suddenly just red all over. For some odd reason, I remembered a time when we were both so young. She wore red shoes then but didn't dress only in dark colors. Her hair was long and straight and blond, but it had yet to taste the honey of dreadlocks. We were so young. I was in fourth grade. We were in the comfort of our neighborhood. We were probably watching television.

Then the night lit up. We all rushed outside of our family cocoons and stood transfixed by the unearthly light in the night sky. Our neighbor, Mrs. Sagan, read her Bible in a loud voice so everyone could hear. She ordered us to get on our knees and pray for salvation. The entire night sky jumped with electricity, and Mrs. Sagan yelled and told everyone this was the end of the world, and Jesus was coming to save us all.

She tried to push me down to pray. I just stood there and didn't allow her to push me down. Of course, I didn't know the whole apocalyptic light show was nothing more than an electrical transformer gone haywire.

I didn't know anything about that.

I had never even figured out the mating ritual of the mealworm. How would I know about electricity? I just didn't want to be pushed down to pray. I suppose my third-grade teacher should have added that to my résumé. I could draw birds well; I was too sincere. Sure, guilty as charged. But my teacher should have added I didn't like to be pushed down to the knees of any form of salvation. She really should have included that comment.

So, I just stood there and kept standing there, unbending, just like Belle's beautiful knees, to the holy electricity of the night. Then Liddy looked at me with eyes that begged for help. Liddy never did that, and I always wanted her to do that. So I knelt beside her that night with the electrical transformer exploding into the thick night air and prayed because Liddy wanted me to pray beside her to assuage her fear. I did that. I prayed with Liddy because I knew she was terrified, and I desperately desired to make her less afraid of a world exploding into the darkness of the night—a darkness pushing against our innocent prayers.

I saw Liddy's eyes again the night Moses and Belle were shot while wearing those ridiculous silver suits. I didn't kneel this time. Instead, I ran toward Squeegee because I couldn't look at Liddy's eyes and kneel for a second time. We all wanted Jesus to arrive and save everyone, but Jesus wasn't coming that night, so I ran. I ran like I was praying. I ran with my arms waving madly into the air.

The truth was I didn't need to run. Squeegee had dropped his rifle because he didn't need it anymore. I saw a look in his eyes. He would later claim to the authorities that he was shooting at aliens from another world, that he was frightened beyond the point of rational thought. He would claim temporary insanity. I saw the look in his eyes, and that look indicated he knew exactly what he was doing. Yes, he did. I saw it. I know what I saw, and what I saw was not fear.

What I saw was hatred.

Robbie knew exactly what he was doing, and he knew I understood the hatred in his eyes.

a Different Moses

UNCLE HO NEVER SAID A WORD about what Squeegee did to Moses. He didn't say a word in Vietnamese or French. He certainly didn't say a word in English. Uncle Ho was just an old man. He was, we all believed, the uncle of Moses and Elvis. Their real parents, it seemed, never found the landing gear of some American helicopter on which to hang their future.

Of course, Uncle Ho wasn't his real name, but very little about Vietnam was ever very real. We just called him that because he was an old Vietnamese man who looked like Ho Chi Minh, the leader of those Communists we so desperately hated. He had the old clothes and the beard, so that was good enough for us. He was Uncle Ho to everybody, but really he was the grandfather of Moses and Elvis.

Though Uncle Ho and the other Vietnamese in our community said nothing about Squeegee, the death of Moses was front-page and café news. I knew the truth. I had seen Squeegee's eyes, and that made all the conversations I heard more pathetic. I knew the truth while everyone else just guessed like they were choosing numbers in a super-ball lottery bonanza while buying a pack of Camel cigarettes in a modern gas station like a Kwik Trip convenience store.

A DIFFERENT MOSES

The Saturday after the shooting, I was sipping coffee while reading the local paper in Café Small Talk. I didn't feel like talking to anybody.

The waitress said to anyone listening, "How about those Packers?"

This was a logical thing to say because it was August, and the preseason games were ending. Bart Starr was head coach, and optimism—like the smell of paper pulp—filled the autumn air.

She poured some guy a cup of coffee.

"Just beat the Bears in the opener," the guy said. "Just beat the Bears. That's all I care about." Usually, the café talk was limited to Packer highlights. After all, this was Green Bay. Suddenly the guy whose life depended perhaps a bit too much on Packer victories over the Bears, just said, "What about that kid?"

We all knew what "that kid" meant. There was only one kid in the recent news. Squeegee was one of us, and the dead Vietnamese guy wasn't one of us.

I took a bite of my doughnut.

"He didn't do nothing I didn't do in Vietnam," a guy in a hunting T-shirt said. "And I never spent a minute in jail for killing any—" He paused and thought about his words. Then he said, "For killing them."

He wanted to say "gooks." We all knew the word. *Gooks.* We all heard the word. *Gooks.* But he didn't say it. I guess it was about to be morning in America again. I felt the breeze of the upcoming Reagan Revolution. This was August. Jimmy Carter was an unpopular president for all sorts of reasons. There were hostages in Iran, and he had refused to use American force against the Sandinistas in Nicaragua. Interest rates were higher than Jerry Garcia, and we all secretly knew that the Packer season was going to be yet another bust.

THE GOSPEL ACCORDING TO DARA

In November, Ronald Reagan would be elected president by a landslide. It might as well have been the day after the election as far as I could tell from the conversation.

"He didn't do nothing that Reagan's not going to do to those Iranians," the coffee guy said.

A third man at a corner table winced. He must have been among the last of the liberals in America.

"We should have turned Vietnam into a parking lot," the hunter suggested. "That's what Reagan said he would have done there. Turn the damn place into a parking lot!"

"Well," the waitress said as she poured the coffee guy another cup, "the kid's only fifteen or something. He didn't know what he was doing."

I spit up a combination of coffee, doughnut, and the Constitution. Everybody gave me a wary glance.

"Yeah," the coffee guy said. "And what are they doing dressing up like space invaders from another planet?"

"I would have shot them too," the hunter said.

The liberal guy winced again.

Thankfully, the waitress tried to be a bit more civil. "Is there a law against it?"

"Against what?"

"Shooting aliens from outer space."

The hunter guy shook his head. "Laws!" he said. "You can't shoot this, and then you can't shoot that. Then something else is on some damn list you can't shoot."

"You can't even make a list because you ain't got the paper. You know. You can't cut trees down because some owl lives in one of them," the coffee guy said, as he motioned for another cup.

"But can you?" the waitress insisted.

A DIFFERENT MOSES

"Can you what?"

"Shoot people from outer space if they land in your backyard?"

"I'll shoot anybody in my backyard. It's called trespassing."

"That's the problem," the coffee guy said. "Take my gun away and I ain't free anymore."

"Yeah. I like that Moses guy," the hunter said. "He wants everybody to have a gun."

My God. I had to wince. Squeegee shot Moses.

"What's that Moses guy's name?" the hunter asked.

"Charlton Heston," the liberal guy in the corner suggested.

"Yeah, him," the hunter agreed.

"But can you really shoot an alien from outer space?" the waitress asked again.

"Why not?" the coffee guy asked.

"It might be all right to wear a costume on Halloween night," the waitress said, and then continued, "but this is August." She paused in a moment of serious coffee-shop doubt. "What if those Vietnamese people have a different Halloween day? How would we know?"

The hunter just laughed. "I was in Vietnam for more than a year," he said. "And I saw strange stuff. But I never saw any gook in a costume. Then he looked around and corrected himself. "I never saw a single Vietnamese kid trick-or-treating. I never saw nothing like that. They were always begging and stealing all the time. But they never were trick-or-treating."

"Well, that's good." She seemed relieved.

It was comforting to know our Moses, who held Belle's hand as he was shot, wasn't trick-or-treating. That was enough for me. I paid my bill and left. The liberal guy left at the same time and held the door for me.

"Thanks," I said. "Bunch of idiots in there."

"I don't know. Bunch of idiots out here, too."

"What do you mean?"

His eyes became soft and reflective. "I saw *Woodstock*, you know."

"You were there?" I asked eagerly.

"No." He shook his head. "I saw it. I saw the movie. I saw the movie on the first night it played. I bought all the right music too. The Who. 'Won't Get Fooled Again.' You know. The Airplane. 'Volunteers.' Simon and Garfunkel. 'America.'" He paused. "Do you know that one?"

I nodded. Of course, I knew that one.

"That's what we all did. We went looking for America. Do you know what we all found?"

I didn't say a word.

"We all found that." He pointed to a brand-new BMW parked outside the café. I noticed that his parking meter was expired. "And do you know what else we found?"

Again, I didn't say a word.

"We found that we liked that." He paused. "In fact, we found that we liked that way too much."

"So, you're voting for Reagan, too?" I had to ask.

His eyes looked back at the people still in the café. "No." he said. "I'll probably do what I did in there."

"Drink coffee?" I asked with a hint of sarcasm.

"Yeah," he said. "Drink coffee and say nothing. Just let them have their way. It's going to happen. Not much I can do about it."

"I saw you wince once or twice."

"Thank goodness I can still do that," he said, as he pushed a control on his key chain that opened the doors to his fancy BMW.

"See you in America," I said.

He smiled. "See you in Iran."

A DIFFERENT MOSES

I had to ask one more question. "Do you still listen to all those records?"

"Sure," he said with sarcasm worthy of my own.

I watched the reflection of his BMW in the glass window of the coffee shop as it drove away into America's brand-new morning.

a Costume Party

UNCLE HO ATTENDED THE TRIAL. Well, it wasn't a symbolic trial like Kafka's *Trial*, and it certainly wasn't a circus like O.J. Simpson's trial. It wasn't really a trial at all. It was just a big hearing during which the legal experts tried to figure out exactly what happened when Moses and Belle were shot.

I waited for Uncle Ho as he approached the courthouse. Elvis was at his side. It was difficult not to look at the missing part of Elvis' arm. It's hard not to notice something that is no longer there; we all take things in their proper place for granted.

"I'm sorry," I said to Uncle Ho. "I was there."

Elvis spoke. "He doesn't know any English."

"I don't know any Vietnamese," I confessed.

Uncle Ho said something rather long-winded in Vietnamese to his grandson. Elvis translated, "My grandfather says he thanks you for coming here today and telling what you saw. He says he doesn't know how he will be able to tell his son that this thing happened. My grandfather also says he is such an old man, and he should have known about things like this. He knows Americans shot the Vietnamese before, but he didn't think they would shoot them here in America. He says his grandson was not Vietcong. He was never VC, so he shouldn't have been shot."

A COSTUME PARTY

Well, I couldn't argue with that.

I looked at the old man and tried to smile. I wondered for a moment if I could learn how to say something sarcastic in the Vietnamese language. I wanted to do that. All I managed to say was, "America is a great and beautiful country with many great and lovely people, but some Americans aren't very nice." I said this so slowly the old guy probably thought I was the village idiot. He still nodded his head several times and patted me on the shoulder with genuine Vietnamese affection.

He was a kind old fellow who would fit well into the landscape of the America I loved and so desperately wanted him to have for his family. This was an America of cornfields, cows, red barns, and Wisconsin people who stop when a car is stuck on the side of the road.

One time, I was stranded on the highway because of a failed transmission. I popped the hood and looked miserable for only a matter of seconds before two drivers stopped and offered a ride. One offer came from an elderly couple wearing excessively large sunglasses. The other offer came from a giggly voice inside a Toyota Camry stuffed with laughing teenaged girls in cutoff jeans preferring to ride with bare feet dangling out of the windows. Freedom of choice, indeed! Thank God for the Bill of Rights!

I felt truly bad, as several of the young women with those cutoff shorts had to move their legs and feet to make room for me.

I wanted Uncle Ho to meet these kind and happy people. I desperately wanted to take this gentle old man to a roadside diner so he could listen to the deep pride in the voices of the people here who grew crops, fixed engines, and drove trucks. There are truckers who will voluntarily take the time to transport a dog from an animal shelter to its new home hundreds of miles away. That's Wisconsin. I truly believe that would happen anywhere in America. That's what I wanted to show Uncle Ho.

People make beer in Wisconsin. They love to drink it and eat brats as they watch their Green Bay Packers play football. Sunday afternoon is heaven on Earth, even if our Packers don't win the game. I wanted the old man to know that. I wanted him to know the cold weather, the kind of cold that tastes like frozen cellophane and stuns the very thought of a breath in the crisp air. I wanted him to love the snow that is so beautiful when it falls in thick flakes that float like notes played from an organ during a Christmas mass. I wanted him to know my Wisconsin, my America.

I wanted to tell him about sixteen-year-old Henry Thumm, who politely requested the local school board treat his religious beliefs with respect guaranteed in the Constitution. Henry was the practicing Greek Mythologist who had a no-joke altar to Poseidon in his basement.

And I wanted to tell Uncle Ho about Helen Turnkee, a teacher at our high school who defied the school board by quietly moving her Greek mythology unit to the nonfiction part of her curriculum when they refused Henry's request for religious tolerance.

I wanted to tell him how wonderful it was to grow up in Wisconsin. I wanted to walk with him down State Street in Madison when the Badgers played on a Saturday. I wanted him to know about the very first snowflake in an October sky. He needed to see the soft footprints a midnight rabbit had left in the fresh snow. I wanted him to see the first drip from an evergreen's bud in the spring. I wanted the old man to know about Wisconsin's beauty—a lovely prayer never asked, but in the landscape of every moment, always answered.

A COSTUME PARTY

Unfortunately, all this aged Vietnamese man knew was his grandson had been shot to death while he walked across a yard in a silver suit and pretended to be an alien from outer space. He didn't know about my world. The red color of my beautiful barns only conjured the memory of blood, and the cold cellophane air in my world would be forever melted with the hot tracer fire of Squeegee's semiautomatic rifle.

As I said, the trial of Squeegee Robbie Reynolds wasn't really a trial at all. It was more of a quiet investigation, a very quiet investigation buried in a newspaper committed to Packer training-camp news. Surprisingly, most of the high-powered lawyer logic was much the same as I heard in Café Small Talk. The defense lawyers said Squeegee, who suddenly became Robert Reynolds, was a minor, and he should be treated as such. The high-powered lawyers had dressed Robert—formally known as Squeegee—in a dapper three-piece suit and made darn sure he had an expensive haircut. Squeegee Roswell Robbie had been suddenly transformed into a *summa cum laude* Harvard graduate.

His attorneys said Robert was scared because he believed these costumed trespassers were aliens who were attacking his United States of America. They claimed he acted out of fear, and this was just like the Orson Welles *War of the Worlds* radio broadcast invasion—only their client *saw* alien invaders. That was the reason he shot them.

The lawyers brought to the stand an old woman who had listened to the radio broadcast in 1938. She testified that she had been truly frightened and had believed that Martians were attacking our planet.

THE GOSPEL ACCORDING TO DARA

The judge nodded as he listened to her words.

I glanced at Uncle Ho. As I watched him, he instructed Elvis to read his textbook, which was probably his homework. I looked closely and saw it was an American history text titled *America: The Land and Its Promise*. I think all American history texts are called something like that. Elvis managed to turn the page with his injured arm.

In the meantime, Squeegee's lawyer said kids not much older than his client had been sent to Vietnam and had killed Vietcong every day. He said these kids were given medals for doing this sort of thing. They, like young Robert, had defended America. Then he added there was no law that dealt specifically with shooting aliens from outer space, and that was exactly what his client had done.

The kid was scared, he said. He had defended American soil. Then the high-powered lawyer spoke with a catch in his throat to proclaim with unctuous sincerity that young Robert would, at other times in American history, be given a medal for his valor, for his minuteman readiness, and for his courageous tenacity in a very difficult situation.

They called Liddy to the stand and asked her all sorts of questions. She had dressed for the hearing in a somewhat formal black suit. Her blond dreadlocks were pulled back. I thought she looked beautiful. I noticed she wore her high-topped tennis shoes. It was then I realized she looked even more beautiful. I loved those shoes, and I loved the fact that she wore them to court.

Unfortunately, as she testified, it became apparent she had seen nothing of importance. Sure, she had seen Belle's legs get shot out from under her, and she had seen Moses' head as the bullet struck, but she had not looked at Squeegee as he had fired the shots. Everyone already knew that Squeegee had killed Moses.

A COSTUME PARTY

The hearing was really about the kid's intent at the moment he pulled the trigger. So Liddy was politely dismissed, high-topped tennis shoes and all.

Then they called me to the stand.

I raised my right hand, and I told them the truth. I think it's important to tell the truth. I said that I saw the look in Squeegee's eyes. I said the look told me he knew exactly what he was doing.

They asked me what I thought he was doing.

I answered by saying Squeegee saw his chance to shoot a Vietnamese kid who was holding hands with a white girl as they walked across his backyard while wearing silver alien space suits. I testified to a look in his eyes that told me he knew exactly what he was doing. I told them he just wanted to kill the guy. He wanted to kill the guy because he was Vietnamese and was holding hands with a white woman who was also dressed in a silver alien space suit. I begged to swear on their Bible again.

They said it wasn't necessary.

The lawyer asked me my name.

I said, "Joshua Toss."

I looked into the courtroom and saw my mother sitting with all the people who had come to watch the hearing. She had insisted I wear a suit. I think she came just to see me in a suit, something she didn't get to see very often.

"Well, Mr. Toss, have you ever written a song?" Squeegee's lawyer asked.

I said that I did.

"And was it," he asked, "titled 'White Gold'?"

I agreed it was—that it was called "White Gold." I glanced at my mother. Believe me, she knew about the oleo smuggling. She's the one who put the illegal stuff in the trunk of our family's Dodge.

"And did," he asked, "and did this song openly advocate the liberal use of an illegal substance?"

I looked at my dear mother. I said, "That's one way of looking at it."

"And what is, as you say, 'one way of looking at it'?"

I knew what the guy wanted. "It was never about drugs," I said. "It only sounded like it."

"And," the lawyer continued, "did you find that sarcastic?"

"No," I answered. "I found it funny."

"What exactly is the difference?"

"Well," I said, "I guess something that's funny is funny, and something that's sarcastic is sarcastic."

My poor mother winced—like the liberal guy in the coffee shop.

"I suppose you find your answer funny?" he asked.

"Not really," I told him. "It's more sarcastic."

The lawyer did a really great impersonation of the television attorney Perry Mason and spoke to the judge. "It is axiomatic that Mr. Toss holds us all in some kind of sarcastic contempt. It is apparent his opinion of what happened that night holds no credence whatsoever. And how could my client possibly know the secret and hidden identities of these alien impostors if they were, indeed, disguised in their silver space suits?"

Now that was a good question, and I really didn't have a good answer. "I just know," I said, "that I saw his eyes."

"His eyes?"

"Yes. I saw Squeegee's eyes, and they told me what he was thinking."

"Well," the high-powered lawyer said, "if that's the case, look into Robert's eyes right now and tell me what he's thinking."

"It doesn't work that way. That night was different."

115

A COSTUME PARTY

"Please, Mr. Toss. Try. Look into his eyes."

I guess I had to say something. So I just said what I felt. I said, "I suppose he's thinking he is sure glad he doesn't have to tell the truth or put his hand on a Bible. I bet he's happy I have to be honest because it's really a difficult thing to do." I paused. "Give me your Bible again. Better yet, give him your Bible. Make him talk. Make him swear on your Bible. Make him swear on anybody's Bible."

Squeegee Roswell Robbie Robert Reynolds simply stared into the air of the courtroom sporting his expensive haircut and really nice suit.

Truthfully, I saw absolutely nothing in his eyes at that moment. Quite frankly, I still can't tell which of the two was more frightening — his hateful eyes when he shot Moses and Belle, or his eyes in the court when they were devoid of any guilt or empathy or compassion for anyone else in the world. The thought of those eyes in that courtroom still scares me, like the stuff of nightmares. There was a judicious silence. I was hoping for a commercial break so I could go get a can of Diet Coke and use the bathroom.

"I have one more question," the lawyer said.

"Then I'll have one more answer," I replied.

"More sarcasm?" he asked.

"No." I knew that I should keep my mouth shut, but I just said, "No, I was just trying to be funny."

"Whatever," he brushed my comment aside. "Who sang your drug song?"

"It wasn't a drug song. It was about oleo."

"That's right. All right. Allow me to rephrase the question. Who sang the 'White Gold' oleo song?"

I knew what he wanted. "Moses," I said. "Moses sang the

song." It was the truth.

"So the victim wasn't just some poor kid in love." He paused for effect, just like on television. "Moses, our supposed victim, was also prone to sarcasm, oleo running, and perhaps, due to his limited understanding of the words to your song, drug use."

I just laughed. I knew I shouldn't laugh. But I laughed like I had just heard the greatest comedian deliver his best joke on the Tonight Show. I'm still sorry about the laugh, but I also believe that if I hadn't laughed I would have vomited on the whole interrogation. I didn't want to vomit, so I laughed.

Then I was asked to step down and wasn't asked anything else.

The high-powered lawyer, however, said many more things. He suggested that his client never meant to fire the gun. He suggested Squeegee just meant to frighten us, as we had frightened him. An eye for an eye. He also suggested that, in actuality, his client, Robert Reynolds, had committed no crime at all, that he may have really believed our planet was under attack. He asked the judge to examine the laws. There is no legal agreement as to how we should treat aliens from another planet, or galaxy, for that matter. He insisted we have seen them on television. We have heard people testify they have been abducted and who knows what else. We have all heard the stories about these aliens from other worlds who have dissected humans, but there is no law guiding our own defense against these abductions. So the fault, he said, was not "in the stars" but in our own failure—the failure of our legislators to enact real laws to allow us all to protect ourselves.

He might have finished with the word "Amen" or "God bless America." I don't remember.

As he was talking, I thought for a moment about all the

people who have been killed in America. Aaron Burr shot Alexander Hamilton, who made it onto our $10 bill. I thought about Abraham Lincoln, whose politics were our Civil War, but ultimately they were of compassion. He was shot. John Fitzgerald Kennedy was shot and killed in Dallas, Texas. He was a president who spoke of great dreams.

His brother was shot, too.

I will always remember the summer morning when I heard Bobby Kennedy was shot and killed. My mother told me the sad news. He was murdered shortly after he had talked to a big crowd of people who were angry because Martin Luther King, a pacifist, had been shot and killed in Memphis, Tennessee. Bobby Kennedy told the angry crowd that his brother had also been killed by a white man. Those were noble words. They were words that had absolutely nothing to do with sarcasm. His words spoke of wisdom and compassion; his gentle words fell softly between the cacophonous notes of assassins' bullets.

In December 1980, John Lennon, one of The Beatles, would be assassinated. Of course, I didn't know this as I listened to Squeegee's lawyer pontificate and create a case for reasonable doubt in someone's mind. I will always remember driving right through a red light when I heard the news of Lennon's death on my car's radio. A traffic cop stopped me, and I told him I just had to go through the red light as a sudden and irrational response to the murder of John Lennon. The cop had not heard the awful news, and I saw a tear well up in his eye.

He let me go without even a warning.

He shook my hand and told me to take it easy.

I guess love was all any of us needed that sad December night. People would continue to be shot in America. Ronald Reagan, the man who would soon be elected President of the

United States, would be shot.

Not all of the people who get shot, it should be said, are famous enough to get portrayed on our money. For instance, I really can't recall the names of any of the students killed at Kent State. That's a shame. A local Green Bay police officer, Tim Paine, was shot during a routine patrol. At his funeral, some idiots sang "I Shot the Sheriff." I love Bob Marley's music, but I could never stomach listening to that song again. It's a big deal for about an hour when a cop is killed on a television show, but real life is much less sympathetic. My grandfather, however, was lucky. He was not famous, nor was he a victim of American violence. He told a story about coming to America to avoid the trenches of World War I. He had hitchhiked to some port in Germany from his native Poland and arrived in Wakefield, Michigan, unable to read, speak, or write English. He couldn't even read his native Polish.

A traffic cop ordered my grandfather to follow him. Years later, Grandpa told me he was certain the cop was going to shoot him because that's what happened in his old country. Instead, my grandfather was taken to a place where they gave him a job in the iron mines. This was America, my grandfather was told, and then the policeman shook his hand, just like the traffic cop shook my hand after I went through a red light because John Lennon had been murdered.

As I said, many people have been shot in America, but my grandfather was not one of them. He was given a job. He was given a new life.

That's the America I love.

A COSTUME PARTY

The lawyer was still talking, a job for which he was well paid. He said his client, Robert Reynolds, was a victim of the evening news. He had watched so many people being gunned down that he perhaps felt compelled to do the same thing. He was a victim of the violence he had seen every night on television. I had watched the very same violence. I almost believed him.

The lawyer lifted his high-powered finger with a high-powered gesture and proclaimed that Robert Reynolds had done the American thing. We had all shot at Bunker Hill, he said. We had all shot at the Alamo. We had all shot when Hitler threatened the free world. He said what Robert had done, we had also done. We, too, the lawyer claimed, had pulled the trigger. "And never forget," he concluded, "Robert Reynolds did attend, and pass with special merit, the hunter safety course as required by Wisconsin law." Then he rested his argument.

Squeegee Roswell Robbie Robert Reynolds had never said a word.

It was painfully obvious this glove, akin to that in the O.J. Simpson trial some years hence, was just never going to fit. I just laughed, and I kept on laughing until my sides ached. Then, for some odd reason, I stopped. Perhaps I had laughed myself into some weird form of sobriety.

As I left the hearing, Elvis, Moses' brother, stopped me and said his grandfather wanted to say thanks.

"For what?" I asked.

"For telling the truth," he said.

I glanced at his missing arm.

His grandfather said something to him in Vietnamese. His words were simple, and though I didn't speak Vietnamese, I somehow understood what the old man had to say. It was like listening to free jazz. It was strange, but I somehow knew every note he played. The sad old man told me, "In my old country, they never promised us any sort of freedom. If they had promised freedom, they would have meant it." Then the old man looked at me intently and said, "But your country promises freedom, but they never mean it."

I thought about my own grandfather as I looked at this old man. I didn't know what to say. What could I say? What could anyone say? I watched sadly as he left the hearing with no traffic cop to shake his hand. With his one good arm, Elvis still clutched his history textbook.

The title still read, *America: The Land and Its Promise.*

Liddy
Appleseed

LIDDY DIDN'T BOTHER TO CHANGE HER CLOTHES before planting the new tree—an oak for Moses—next to all the others. She still wore the dark suit and the high-topped tennis shoes she wore at the hearing. I was really glad she wore those shoes. The knees of her pantsuit were muddy, but I don't think she cared. I certainly didn't care. I thought her muddy knees were lovely. I watched as she planted a new oak tree, and as she caressed the new growth, she looked as if she were praying.

She wasn't religious.

I knew that.

She was a protest punk rocker, but she genuinely hoped for the young tree's growth. Perhaps that was the same thing as a bona fide prayer.

"They called it just a sad accident," she said, "so Squeegee gets away with murder."

I didn't say a word.

Liddy's tears were deep round drops, each with a fleck of a rainbow bit—a fleck falling on the tiny oak tree with all the beauty of a baptism.

"So Moses is dead, and Belle," she paused. "Belle's in such pain. I haven't even been able to see her. They are worried about infection." She paused again. "Josh. They say she may never walk again. She might even lose her legs."

I still didn't say anything at all. I remembered Belle in her dress at Mrs. Fletcher's funeral.

Liddy lifted her arms. "Mrs. Fletcher is gone, and the music is all gone, and Otis is dead. They're going to come and cut down all these trees. Why did I even bother to plant this little guy for Moses? They're going to cut everything down. Eloise. Noah. Erna. They're all going to get cut down. Reagan is going to be elected president. Paul. Thecla. Mrs. Fletcher's tree. Peter. They're all as good as gone. I always thought I'd have the guts to scream and protest, but maybe I don't have those guts anymore. Maybe I never did."

Then she hugged me.

And I hugged her back.

It occurred to me to add to her list of disasters a comment about the Green Bay Packers and their impending disaster of a season, but I kept my stupid sarcastic mouth shut.

I should have walked to my house and brought a garden rake to level the dirt around the tiny oak tree, but at this moment of my life, I did not know about the Big Bang Sale on the final day of Mr. Raymond's hardware store. So I didn't understand about giving garden implements away for free. Nevertheless, it would have been a decent thing to do for Liddy. It would be a decent thing to do for anyone.

I just stood there with my arms around her, the dirty knees of her suit pressed against my legs. I hoped my pants would become dirty, too. High-powered lawyers, on the other hand, never get their clothes dirty. They get manicures and fancy haircuts every week because they have to look good, and they buy expensive shoes and ties. I preferred my clothes dirty.

"You know," I said, "planting that tree for Moses was probably illegal."

"Illegal like smuggling oleomargarine across the Wisconsin border?" she asked. She beat me at my own game. That happens sometimes.

"Yeah," I said, "illegal like that."

"Then you helped," she suggested.

"Yeah, I know."

In a weird way, those were the words of love.

I stood there holding Liddy. She wasn't Lydia at that moment. She was definitely my Liddy. It started to rain because nature often blows summer raindrops in late August. Liddy's beautiful blond dreadlocks were wet. Her dark suit dripped with rainwater, and as she stepped away, small raindrops fell between us. Something inside of me desperately desired to catch those raindrops in the palm of my hand, but I just allowed them to drip sadly to the ground.

Smaller even Raindrops

ONE PERSON SAID, "The kid is only fifteen years old. He didn't know what he was doing." Someone else said that the Vietnamese people probably didn't celebrate Halloween, so there was no reason for the costumes. That seemed to be a popular excuse.

I heard it all.

I heard it everywhere.

I heard it through the grapevine.

I heard enough.

I heard people say the kid really thought he was under attack by aliens, and they said he was perfectly justified in shooting the kids who were dressed in silver space suits with suction-tipped fingers. I heard more than enough. It didn't make any difference. As I said, this was a glove that was just never going to fit.

Then they came for our trees.

The machinery of power was already in place, always ready, like a guillotine's razor edge, hidden behind the curtain of an unused voting booth. Thomas Goast preferred any headline argument buried by the fever of some other news story. City Hall worries about headline news.

EVEN SMALLER RAINDROPS

Power was everything to Thomas Goast, but I wasn't so certain about Franklin Fletcher. There was something distant in his eyes. A Vietnam jungle haunted him, and for that, I could never really find fault. I didn't have to go to Vietnam. He did. So I could only try to understand his desire to cut down every bit of jungle growth that fueled his fear.

God bless him.

God help him.

Thomas Goast was different. He was the kind who enjoyed watching bodies stiffen as they hung from the gallows. This, to him, was equivalent to putting the period under the exclamation mark. If we still had the gallows, he may even have poked the convicted body as it was hanging in the air. He was the kind who liked to watch napalm explosions in the jungle on television. He would cage his victim rather than kill him—just to touch the key in his pocket.

Thomas Goast made darn sure there were trucks to haul away the debris of Noah and Eloise after they were cut down. He was the kind of guy who double-checked his plans, and he wanted those trucks there. He wanted those trucks there on time. He wanted those trucks there on *his* time.

God forgive him.

Of course, Thomas Goast had thought of every detail, and that's where the devil will hang his hat. There were large saws in the bed of one of the city trucks, and the chipper would take care of everything else. The Day of Judgment had come for those two old trees and all of their family of old oaks. I cringed, just like my dear mother had cringed in the courtroom.

Once, when Otis was still alive, I was standing next to Noah. The wind blew through his branches, and I heard a sound like a groan. It was a human sound. Trees creak and crack when they bend, but they don't groan. At the time, I thought it was just my imagination playing some sort of trick on me.

Another time, when Mrs. Fletcher was still alive, she showed me those scarred places on the trunks of the trees where the two lovers, Noah and Eloise, had long ago carved each other's names. I remembered the feel of that bark as I touched the sacred spots. The tree bark was rough on the tips of my fingers. I wondered if I left fingerprints, or if the tree left bark prints on my fingers. Mrs. Fletcher asked me if I felt the words, if I felt the names. She said Noah had carved "My Dearest Eloise" into the bark, and Eloise had carved Noah's name into her tree. I said yes. I just had to say yes. I would still say yes.

Then I swear I saw the two old oaks spread their branches so wide that they wrapped around one other.

Laugh at me.

Go ahead and laugh at me, but I saw those two old oaks holding hands. Their boughs intertwined just like two lovers who wrapped their silver-space-suit suction fingers around each other in the moment before they were shot.

Once, when Liddy and I were sitting in two chairs in front of all of those oak trees, I wanted to show her those entangled branches. I wanted to show her those two trees holding hands, but I just petted Otis and then scratched his belly. That was the only way I could show my feelings.

EVEN SMALLER RAINDROPS

All the people in our neighborhood stood in frozen-custard despair. I watched helplessly as our government used its machinery against the beauty of its own city. For Pete's sake! For Paul's sake! For Erna's sake! I watched helplessly as the city government was so ready and willing to flex its biceps of authority to prove its power of existence, an existence free and clear of the very people from whom it supposedly derived that existence. And this was America!

Thomas Goast, the man from City Hall who told us this was the way it was going to be, said, "This had to happen because if this didn't happen, then nothing else would ever happen." Our trees had to be cut down. He said, "If they weren't cut down, then other trees couldn't be cut down." It was all a bit like a reverse domino theory of the Vietnam War. We all nodded and watched as they prepared for the execution of Noah and Eloise because we were all too complacent again, just like we had endured the endless ironies of the Vietnam War.

The wind began to blow, and the old oak leaves fluttered. The leaves knew and were waving good-bye. Then the winds began to blow even harder. Franklin looked at the sky. "It's going to rain," he said.

Thomas Goast checked his watch. This meant everything to him. Time often limited everyone else's power. Time even limited nature's power. That's the way he saw the universe. Thomas Goast looked at Franklin. Franklin wavered. Perhaps he had learned from the past. Whatever the reason, he flinched. Thomas Goast never flinched. Of course, he had never fought in the Vietnam War.

I stood inches from Liddy. I didn't want to feel alone anymore, and cutting down these trees would make me feel very alone. The universe kept its distance and the law kept its distance, but Liddy was right beside me. I heard two sounds. One was the high-pitched grinding scream of the chainsaw ready to cut into the hearts of those beautiful old trees. The other sound was that of a Chevy van door opening. Granted, this wasn't exactly the sound of a minuteman's rifle at Concord Bridge or bloody screams on the Kent State campus; but it provided, as only an old Chevy van could provide, the revolutionary sound of an American dream. Suddenly, there were weird people everywhere. Here were all of Liddy's friends, many of them sporting angry dreadlocks. I half expected them to have boxes of tea to throw into some harbor. They were ready to protest!

These impassioned people were suddenly everywhere all at once. Their old van was a well-traveled billboard of their agenda. On one side, hand-scribbled letters read, "BAN THE BOMB!" (Well, that didn't work.) The other side demanded, "IMPEACH NIXON!" (Well, that did work.) Then there were all sorts of other comments: "STOP THE WAR!" (That never works.) "STOP CUTTING OUR TREES!" (Three cheers.) "BURN THE BRA!" (No opinion whatsoever.) "GIVE PEACE A CHANCE!" (Good idea.) "REAGAN? AREN'T YOU ASHAMED!" (Good luck.)

There were others. Layers of paint covered years of protest—like an archaeological dig—waiting and laughing at the limits of humanity's interest in lessons of its own history. It was a Rosetta Stone on which too much graffiti had been written—yet another roadside billboard of such small consequence. Perhaps underneath all the revisions there rested an original copy of *The Rights of Man*.

These were aging hippies. They held up two fingers in the rarified air of their dreams. These were Liddy's friends—old people with young hearts, and young people with angry eyes.

EVEN SMALLER RAINDROPS

All of these people blended into a pulse of protest. For a brief instant, I half expected to see Shirley Jones and the Partridge Family step out of television history and sing "I Think I Love You." That didn't happen. These people meant business, and their business had nothing to do with money. They were like the hairs on old Otis' head.

At least twenty people jumped like paratroopers from that old van. They all wore tie-dyed clothes, but not one of them looked like David Cassidy. They had no intention of being television stars and lip-synching a revolution full of lip-synched revolutionary songs.

Thomas Goast watched all of this like a little Napoleon, surveying his battlefield. This was all a bit of a game to him—a game of dominance, power, winning, and revenge—all at the expense of those who just might defy him. His objective was to capture the queen, checkmate the king, cut the trees, and construct whatever he desired to build.

The protesters had their signs that read, "SAVE ELOISE AND NOAH!" and "CUT GOAST! NOT OUR TREES!" For this fist-shake of protest, more people appeared, dressed liked Druids, the ancient priests who worshipped nature. These Druid people chanted some mysterious-sounding songs, circled a few of the trees, and held hands to form magic rings to protect the sacred spaces between all things.

Some guy with really long hair and a guitar began to sing Woody Guthrie's "This Land Is My Land." The guy had a small amplifier and speaker, so we could all hear him. Small drops of rain began to fall, and the sound those drops made as they struck his guitar added a weird rhythm section giving the tune a Bob Marley reggae beat. The long-haired guy sang Marley's "One Love," followed by "Crucifixion," Phil Ochs' ode to John

THE GOSPEL ACCORDING TO DARA

Kennedy's assassination. Bigger raindrops fell, and the beat grew louder and more infectious. Magic was heavy in the damp air.

Some of the city workers began to sing along, until Thomas Goast stepped forward and glared at them. He had their paycheck in his eyes, so they stopped singing, but the rest of us didn't care. We just sang as the rain continued to fall. The guy with the guitar played the obvious song, "Singing In the Rain," the one Gene Kelly made famous. It was a sublime moment. Everyone, I think, suddenly thought about that exact song, and then the long-haired guy just sang it.

Telepathy, I suppose, is a rare moment of bliss found in a world that doesn't make it a habit of providing such sheer beauty. We all danced and clapped. So he played another song. He played "Stay Free" by The Clash. Our chanting became more like the sound of hungry people who wanted something more than a token handout.

A local sect of Hare Krishna devotees with shaved heads and hand drums began to erect a tent. Quite frankly, I didn't even know we had a local sect of Hare Krishna in the area, but there they were, and they were chanting and dancing in praise of their universal Krishna consciousness. Good for them.

I saw Henry Thumm standing by the Druids. Good old Henry! He attended almost any protest. The kid had a genuine empathy for other people simply because he was denied respect for his beliefs.

There was a woman dressed like Mother Nature, with a big flowing dress and a tiara of flowers and leaves. She gave me a daisy to hold and placed a flower in the nut of the long-haired guy's guitar. Then she ran to one of the city vehicles and abruptly gave the door a good swift kick.

We cheered, so she kicked the door again.

EVEN SMALLER RAINDROPS

Oddly enough, I noticed a rainbow glowing over the trees, even though the rain continued to fall in big, cold, late-summer drops that hurt when they hit me in the face. We were all blinking because the rain was so strong.

Thomas Goast refused to blink like the rest of us. His entire body steamed. Sometimes, natural phenomena and the paranormal manage to coexist and say just about the very same thing. His face fumed, and his body smoked. He marched right up to a group of city workers. In the dark, heavy air, his arm made weird motions that looked like dollar signs from where I stood and watched. One of the workers held a big gas-powered chainsaw. It was almost humorous because, as Thomas Goast talked and pointed to the trees, a foggy bubble seemed to flow from his mouth, just like the conversation in a comic book. His foggy comic-book bubble was really quite dark because he was screaming.

The city worker with the gas-powered chainsaw said something, but his foggy bubble wasn't quite so dark because he wasn't screaming. He was just shaking his head and pointing up at the sky full of rain and rainbows. There were many foggy bubbles, and they were easy to understand. Thomas Goast wanted those trees cut down, but the city workers didn't want to cut the trees because of the rain. Thomas Goast still refused to blink.

The comic-book plot was good. Thomas Goast was getting nowhere with his workers, and his foggy bubble continued to darken and his body continued to steam. Then the story took an interesting twist. I didn't think the combination of the Druids, the sect of chanting Hare Krishna devotees, an actual Greek Mythologist, Mother Earth, the rain and the odd rainbow, the refusal of the city workers, and Thomas Goast's fury could get any better, but believe me, it did. This absolutely beautiful woman started dancing all over the place. She danced right up to the circle of city workers, and she started to take off her clothes.

It wasn't a dirty dance at all. She just did this crazy unearthly dance—like a dervish—and when she had removed all her clothes, she grabbed this scrawny guy, and he started to shake, too. He took off his clothes, so they were both completely naked. The scrawny naked guy had wire-rimmed glasses and a long beard stretching down to his knobby knees. He kept pushing those glasses back into place as he shook and danced like he was in a limbo contest. The naked woman looked like Lady Godiva, except she wasn't riding a horse, while the scrawny naked guy didn't really look like anybody but a scrawny guy with a long beard and no clothes.

They started to sing "I'd Love to Teach the World to Sing," which was a decent song until the soda-pop advertising executives decided to use a hippie anthem to sell cans of Coke all over the world. The scrawny naked guy ran around until finally he stopped running and walked over to me. I was surprised. "You own those trees, don't you?" he asked.

"I don't own them."

"You're trying to save them, aren't you?" The scrawny guy was out of breath.

"Sure."

Then he smiled. "Do you know why we're here?"

"You and that naked woman?" I asked.

"Yeah."

"Well," I had to confess. "You're probably friends of Liddy."

"Liddy? Who's Liddy? Naw. We're just Diggers. There aren't many of us left anymore."

"Diggers?"

"Yeah."

EVEN SMALLER RAINDROPS

"Don't you need clothes?" I asked.

"Of course we need clothes." He looked around the area. "They're here somewhere."

"You don't know where?"

"It doesn't matter where they are. They'll be here when we need them."

The scrawny naked Digger guy told me, "We Diggers don't believe in private property. We don't believe anybody can own anything."

I nodded.

"Yeah. We don't believe in paying taxes or rent to anybody. We just don't believe in money."

I nodded again, but I didn't really mean it. I had always considered the old trees as our old trees. They were never anybody else's old trees. People were trying to cut them down. I didn't like those people. This Digger guy was talking about these old oaks like they were just as much his as ours. I didn't like this idea, either. I didn't even know who this scrawny naked guy with a beard was, except he was talking about taking up a homestead on our land. No. I didn't like that idea at all.

"We Diggers long ago shrugged off the oppressive laws of society, and we live wherever we want to live. We grow what we need. We share, and we help each other."

I continued to nod like I was voting for a political candidate whose name I couldn't even pronounce.

"We live off the land," he said. "We plant seeds and grow our food. We do hard simple work."

For some reason, I thought about the Oklahoma rush for free land. I felt sad and selfish, but I just nodded as the guy kept talking about the Diggers and their revolutionary land grab.

The guy with the guitar sang the Pink Floyd song "Us

and Them."

"So, what do you think?" he finally asked.

"About what?"

"About freedom. We Diggers think the Earth is owned in common and nobody can ever own anything. What do you think about that?"

"Well," I said slowly, "I suppose that's one way to look at it." Quite frankly, I was sick of looking at this skinny naked guy who thought he could pitch a tent under Eloise's branches and grow potatoes next to Erna.

"It sure is," the scrawny naked Digger guy said as he ran into the heavy, cold raindrops with more conviction than clothes. He had the odd determination of old Otis as he chased that final ball one last time. I was envious of them both. I was wet, and I was envious as I watched the guy disappear into the thick air. Apparently, idealism could stretch only so far—unless you are a Digger or an old dog in love with an Irish setter named Dara Ruthie Rose. They were both, I suppose, saints of some sort who didn't give a tinker's damn about canonization.

Thomas Goast grabbed the gas-powered chainsaw from the worker who clearly didn't follow any orders in the middle of the storm. I could hear Goast yell at Franklin, who stood by his side. I saw the steam bubble say he was glad the press hadn't shown up to take any pictures and ask questions.

Then the press arrived.

I cheered. But I wondered what I would say to them. I didn't like talking to cameras. Cameras don't understand sarcasm. However, I was suddenly filled with determination to have my say. Perhaps it was the naked Digger guy. Perhaps it was old Otis. I don't know. I was suddenly ready to tell them about trees that were more than 100 years old. I was suddenly ready to tell them about Otis, the old basset hound who had so desperately needed a haircut. I was ready to tell them this neighborhood park area was rezoned in some shady, clandestine bit of City Hall backroom politics. I was suddenly ready to say that was the way it's always done—because money talks. That's what I was ready to tell the cameras.

They talked to Thomas Goast first, so I had to wait in line. He just smiled in front of the cameras. Yes, it was a City Hall political smile, a polite façade—like Ronald Reagan's grin. He told the press he was doing what he had been told to do. He expressed a sincere sadness that all of these people, and some of them were naked people, had to act with such shameful disregard for the public good. Those were his exact words. I have watched him a thousand times on the television in my mind. When I heard him talk to the local-news people, I felt the desperate need to wash my hands, even though I was standing in the pouring rain.

Then they gave me my television moment—my fifteen minutes of fame. I was really ready to say exactly what I wanted to say. I had rehearsed over and over. Otis. Erna. Eloise. Noah. City Hall. They turned on their cameras.

I was ready.

"So," the television man asked, "you're Joshua Toss?"

"Yeah." I was ready to expose everything to everybody. I just wanted to scream the note from Haydn's symphony and blow the damn wigs off all the rich people as they watched and listened from their cushy seats.

"How long have you been out of rehab?" the reporter asked.

"Rehab?" I was confused.

"How are you doing with your addiction?" the guy asked.

"Addiction?"

"Yeah. You wrote that song called 'White Gold,' didn't you?"

THE GOSPEL ACCORDING TO DARA

I just stared into the camera. My stare was a hard look—with Ray Nitschke eyes. I looked really stupid, like a bad high school yearbook photo. I have played this memory in my head a thousand times, too. Then I just walked away. I couldn't even think of a sarcastic comment to make.

The police arrived, but they didn't come to arrest me. As I turned, I noticed poor Henry Thumm, the practicing Greek Mythologist, being arrested and handcuffed with the Druid people. He was screaming. He yelled, "I'm not a Druid! Honest! I'm a practicing Greek Mythologist! Don't arrest me as a Druid! I'm not a Druid! I've never even been to Stonehenge! I've never even been to England! I've got an altar to Poseidon in my basement! Go and see for yourself! I'm a practicing Greek Mythologist! Think about the Hamadryads! What if someone cut down your tree? Where would you go?"

He was screaming for any form of dignity. The Roman system of justice—crucifixion with its naked nails—denied dignity. After all the religion we have crammed down each other's throats, it would be a decent thought to finally understand a handshake to be far superior to a whip.

Two city workers laughed at him as they stood in the pouring rain. Somebody started to sing "Give Peace a Chance."

Thomas Goast had enough. Not only did he have enough, but he also had the gas-powered chainsaw, so he pulled the starter cord. The chainsaw coughed like a three-pack-a-day smoker. It coughed all those cigarettes into the cold rain. He pulled at the cord again. The engine sputtered to life.

Let there be chainsaw.

The sound was obscene. Lightning flashed. Thunder cracked through the gray sky. Some god somewhere, it seemed, was angry.

EVEN SMALLER RAINDROPS

Thomas Goast shook his fist at the clouds. The guy stood in the midst of this intense summer downpour and fumed at the heavens. If Zeus were there, he didn't care. If Odin were there, he didn't care. If absolutely nothing at all were there, he still would not have cared. Thomas Goast simply stood drenched to his skin holding the chainsaw. He was so angry his words smoked into the air as he spoke.

"You!" he screamed. "You get this damn job done!" Some nameless worker shrugged an American shrug, like an empty vote. Then I heard, "You get up that tree and start cutting those damn branches." He pointed at Eloise. The worker shrugged again. Thomas Goast handed him the chainsaw. Lightning flashed, so I could see only Thomas Goast's mouth and the words telling the worker he would be fired if he didn't cut those damn branches.

The city truck Mother Earth had kicked was positioned under Eloise. The rain poured. I watched sadly as the city worker was lifted into position to cut those lovely antiquated branches, and I watched in horror as the executioner began to dismember Eloise. This executioner was not gentle. An executioner should always be gentle, but this executioner, who was wet and angry, just wanted to go home.

It was really difficult to tell the difference between the whine of the chainsaw and the sound of the angry wind as it protested and passed through the limbs of the old oak tree. I watched as the saw blade cut through Eloise's limb. Its sound was muffled as it tore into the tendons of the aged bark. The fury of the storm increased, and as it passed through the oak's branches, it sounded like the cry of a banshee, certain of her own death. The rain just pelted all of us with its tears of despair.

"She's not a happy woman," someone said.

140

THE GOSPEL ACCORDING TO DARA

Thomas Goast yelled, "You've got five minutes!" He held up his hand with its five fingers. "You've got five minutes to cut all those damn branches, or you are fired!"

Some god spoke again. There was another flash of lightning.

The man with the chainsaw shifted his weight to force the gas-powered blade through the pulp of Eloise's arm. Then, suddenly, the sound of the blade was no longer muffled. The gas-powered engine roared. The blade had severed her limb and cut through to the other side.

The big branch fell to the ground.

Several of the protesters who had not yet been arrested ran to get out of the way. The dismembered tree limb didn't fall very far. The dead branch was entangled in the branches of old Noah. It was difficult to see what happened because the rain was so intense. I swear to this day, I swear in the memory of that cold rain—and I am not a superstitious man—but I swear to this day old Noah reached his own limbs and leaves forward and grabbed Eloise's severed branch right out of the air as it fell. That's what I saw.

"Well, I'll be," the city worker said. "I've never seen anything like that."

Thomas Goast had seen everything, but he was unmoved and determined to take Eloise down. "I want that branch taken out of there!" he yelled. "Get a rope," he yelled again. "Get a rope and take that branch down!"

They tried everything to untangle the branch. Noah's grip was just too strong. They tried rope. They tried some sort of clamp on the rope. They tried a pulley on the rope. Noah just held on. Of course, he held on. The branch was just too twisted in the confusing mass of leaves and twigs and tree limbs.

"She's not budging!" the city worker hollered to those of us on the ground. "I can't see up here," he explained. "It's raining too hard. This old woman is not coming down today! She's a stubborn old lady!"

Thomas Goast cursed. I saw that curse claw its way into the very air we all breathed.

Then Franklin cursed. His curse, too, was a blasphemy of breath—like dirty smokestack emissions.

All right!" Thomas Goast shouted. "Get down here! We'll wait until the storm is over. It can't last forever! Then we'll cut that old woman down!"

Everyone decided to wait in the cold rain, but the rain didn't stop. Those raindrops could have been a punk rock band. They spat at us. They laughed at us and didn't care. Those raindrops were just punk pogo dancers dancing on our dilemma. All the city workers retreated to their city trucks. I noticed all the doors were dented.

Liddy shivered as she stood beside me. We were both wet and cold. We had wet and cold between us. My arm curled around her coat and pressed against her shoulder. It was an awkward hug. So we waited. The rain refused to stop.

I looked at Liddy. We still had the wet and cold between us. Her hair was hard and plastered against the sides of her face. Her nose was a bit too large for her face. Tiny drops of mascara dripped down her cheeks. I noticed a small scar on her chin. I knew that scar. I had so many memories, and all those memories somehow included her face with that nose and those cheeks and that chin. We had the wet and the cold to share. Even smaller raindrops fell between us.

The storm lasted longer than Thomas Goast's patience. He began to pace like a hyena desperately wanting everybody to stop watching him. I think he truly desired to impress Franklin, but let's face it, Franklin fought in Vietnam; he had witnessed much more than an old tree and a storm.

One of the city workers suddenly screamed. The guy pointed to another man's protective helmet. "That's blood!" he screamed. "That's blood! That old tree is dripping her blood on us!"

It was true. The man's helmet had dark red spots on it—the color of an Irish setter reflecting its beauty in the sunshine of a deep summer afternoon. We stood in the rain. Those spots were thick, and they dripped very slowly onto the yellow City Hall helmet.

"That's just tree sap!" someone else yelled. "It's falling from that cut branch. That's all it is!"

Franklin stared at the deep red spots.

Thomas Goast saw his moment. Perhaps he was consumed with a gaping hunger, and this moment happened to be the cheapest thing on the menu. Anyway, I saw something I remember in living color even today. I dream about this stuff. I really don't want to remember it. Sometimes, I just don't have the choice. Dreamers can't pick the parental-guidance rating of their nightmares.

I watched as Thomas Goast, in that huge, hungry moment, grabbed the chainsaw from the city worker. He didn't even bother to ask for it. He didn't even threaten the poor guy. Maybe he was just sick to death about all the gasoline being wasted with that thing constantly running and whining. "Damn it!" he cursed. I saw that cartoon bubble. "Trees don't bleed in my city until I tell them it's time to bleed!"

As he grabbed the chainsaw, I swear the blade nicked his hand. I swear. I saw the incision, but the guy didn't bleed. No. Maybe the rain just washed it all away too quickly. Pontius Pilate did the same thing.

EVEN SMALLER RAINDROPS

We the people all prefer to wash our hands of the filth we know, the sad television stuff, the numbing stuff, the crying stuff, the poor stuff, the dead stuff, the infested stuff, the begging stuff, the people-working-in-sweat-shops stuff. We the affluent people all wear some sort of rich wig, and we all sit on some sort of cushy seat; we all wash our hands, just like Thomas Goast, and then we eat our supper. That's what we all do, and that's what Thomas Goast did in the midst of that voracious moment. He allowed the rainwater to wash the drops of blood from his hands.

I glanced at my own hands. I thought about Elvis. He had but one hand from which to wash the blood. Perhaps he was less guilty than the rest of us because he only had that one hand.

Thomas Goast was a determined man, but his wellspring was vastly different from that of the Digger guy or old Otis. He was the kind of man who said he was going to cut down trees and get things done. Sometimes, those determined men are worth a few accolades; but more often than not, those men are just fools who hang around long enough to do stupid things and are lucky enough to end up on the right side of our collected mythology, and we etch these people on our coins or print their faces on our stamps and name big buildings and airports in their honor. Then they become our fiction, which rises from the sleep of death to become our fact.

Most of the city workers had seen enough. They had seen the lightning; they had seen the dark red spots on the helmet; they had seen one old oak tree grip his lover's limb and simply refuse to let it go. They had simply seen enough, and they wanted nothing more than to go home, like the final helicopters leaving Saigon without a concern for peace or honor, without anything other than disgust with the whole affair.

144

THE GOSPEL ACCORDING TO DARA

I watched Thomas Goast as he fumed. Years later, during America's liberation of Kuwait, I watched televised images of Kuwait's oil fields as they spewed black filthy smoke over our desert. Thomas Goast was something like one of those oil derricks in the desert. He was a general whose army would no longer follow his command, so he grabbed the chainsaw and charged his enemy. Some people get a medal of honor for such actions. Sometimes, I suppose, it's really difficult to separate a hero from a madman. But I knew. I did not want him to take one more step toward a medal of any kind.

Of course, my preference didn't stop him. Everything grew very dark in an instant. The air was electric. Bits of hair stood erect on every scalp. There were all sorts of hand gestures into the wind. There was spittle and mud and too many exclamation points that punctuated all the conversations with punches.

Through all the commotion, I saw the sepia images of old Noah cutting the name of Eloise into the bark of the tree, and I saw Eloise do the very same for her love into the bark of the other oak. I blinked, and they were gone. I blinked again, and the rain was thick, the leaves were swirling in the cold wind, and Liddy grabbed my hand so hard that my fingers ached.

Thomas Goast moved in slow motion. I will always remember that. It was the same when old Otis died. Happy memories are so short-lived, and terrible memories always take much too long. Terrible memories fill up nasty dreams. That man, Thomas Goast, moved with deliberate hatred. He paid attention to every detail of his cursed behavior because every detail was important to him. I was an unwilling witness. I was a sad witness to every detail of his crime.

I watched the Vietnam War, and in time, I would watch the Iraq War. Then I would watch the Iraq War again.

EVEN SMALLER RAINDROPS

America loves reruns. They are the lifeblood of cable TV.

One time, Lucille Ball was trapped by a gigantic loaf of bread. Another time, the Fonz, of *Happy Days* fame, passed a history test—without cheating. Jerry Seinfeld dated a virgin while he and his friends had a contest. Reruns make us all gods of TV land. We know all the lines, and we know the endings. As I said, we watched one Iraqi War, and then we watched another Iraqi War. Sometimes, I must confess, it is difficult to know if the picture on the TV screen is an episode of *M*A*S*H*—like the one in which Henry Blake dies—or yet another real war when some kid dies, without the offer of his own spinoff situation comedy.

The chainsaw still whined, a war cry against nature. Thomas Goast cursed several times with many exclamation points. I continued to watch as he struck dear Eloise with that chainsaw blade. I could count the wood fragments that were spit into the wet and heavy air. I watched as he shifted his weight to force the churning saw blade into her veins, the very pulp of that old lovely tree.

Lightning flashed—which I remember because it lit up every ring in her old wood. I could count those rings. I was that close. There was absolutely no sarcasm in my world then. I knew only that I loved that tree, and I loved the world and everything in the world more than I thought possible. I loved every one of the rings I counted inside that old oak tree as it suddenly cracked and bowed like a polite thought from long ago brought forth to remind everyone about love, loyalty, and compassion. It was a hoarse voice of a stubborn soul who spit on the pieces of silver thrown at her feet.

Eloise fell forward like President Lincoln when the bullet entered the back of his head. Eloise fell forward and gave way to a little man with a tiny saw, standing in the rain, a little man

146

who set himself against the immensity of a universe, a little man with a tiny saw who thought he could control the stars with the silly horsepower of a chainsaw whose internal combustion engine whined away like a petty child.

Eloise continued to fall. Hers was a slow descent, like an Apollo spacecraft with three parachutes. She was slow and deliberate with her time. She toppled toward the street. She was breaking, and she was dying. After all those years, she was agreeing with death.

The rain turned to ice, which was odd because this was September, and that never happened in Wisconsin. But it did happen, and the rain was so cold. I tried to see everything, but it was difficult. Eloise swayed with near-certain death, but she did not break.

All of a sudden, she just stopped falling.

Huge sheets of rain swept across my field of vision, blinding me. I'll never be able to prove anything, but in truth, I had never seen with such clarity. I know what I saw. Noah reached into the wind and rain and prevented his lover from falling to the ground. He held her like a newly married man carrying his beloved bride across their threshold. Noah's branches gently wrapped themselves around the trunk of his dearest Eloise. Call me stupid, or call me a fool, but I know what I saw.

Once, Mrs. Fletcher had shown me an old sepia photograph of her grandparents, Noah and Eloise, who did not smile in the flash of that bygone moment. They knew. They were wise as nature itself is wise, and they were both stubbornly proud. As I looked through the dense rain, I saw that image. I saw a woman who would never stoop for pieces of silver, and I saw a man who loved that woman because she would never stoop and beg for the attention of some man who only threw silver at her feet.

EVEN SMALLER RAINDROPS

Suddenly, I watched as Thomas Goast vanished into the dirty air, replaced by Stanley, the ghost of the man from long ago who had sought to hold Eloise as his own. It was Stanley who now held the chainsaw and who kicked Noah hard enough to shake a few leaves free from his very top branches. I watched in disbelief; but, indeed, it was Stanley who kicked Noah. Stanley was the one who lifted the chainsaw above his head and cursed loudly enough for any other century to hear, his breath smoky in the cold thick air. His chainsaw descended like Ahab's harpoon, like Satan falling from the heavens; it descended like the final words of the Versailles Treaty, the document that ended the war to end all wars. That chainsaw fell upon the fragile neck of simple human kindness.

Then Thomas, flesh and boiling blood, was there again. Stanley was gone into the ages of hatred. He would wait forever on the precipice of revenge. I blinked into dense rain. Thomas Goast used that chainsaw like an Anglo-Saxon axe. Old Noah groaned and began to sway. Thomas pushed the chainsaw into the very core of that tree's soul. Noah began to bend. Noah began to bleed. He held firm to Eloise's branches, but the weight was just too great, and the cuts were too deep. Both old trees slowly began to collapse.

The rain suddenly stopped, perhaps out of respect. We all watched as those two beautiful old oaks simply fell, their branches still tangled together, like alien-costumed suctioned fingertips intertwined. They fell with a sacred thud as they hit the secularity of the concrete street. They didn't crush anything, but they could have. There were cars and quite a bit of city equipment. They didn't harm anything at all. That's just the way they were—stoic, still refusing to smile in that sepia photograph taken so many years ago.

THE GOSPEL ACCORDING TO DARA

Thomas Goast's victims were down, without defense, and he used this opportunity to sever most of the limbs embracing each other, even in death. He cut everything he could. Then he cut some more. The rain started again, but he continued to cut bits of every tree branch.

Of course, I looked and remembered Mrs. Fletcher's words. Other people looked too. They had heard the rumors, the local mythology. I saw first the exposed rings that circled like the passage of time in the very heart of those two old oaks. The rings were the grooves of the most beautiful record album ever recorded—just begging for a stylus, a needle, offering free admission to any rich man willing to pass through its eye. This music, waxed into the rings of the aged wood, had no interest in the wigs of wealth. I kept looking. I knew then and I know now exactly what I saw, as clearly as King George III saw the signature of John Hancock on the *Declaration of Independence*. I saw those words. On one stump was carved the word "Noah." The other simply read, "My Dearest Eloise."

The police and the city workers began to push everyone away. They didn't want anyone to see anything at all. There was a commotion, and in that commotion a camera flashed.

Let there be light.

It was like the flash of creativity, the big-bang giveaway. It was the flash of the final sale of a family hardware store. One picture—just one flash picture—what a picture it was! That scrawny naked Digger guy with wire-rimmed glasses and a long beard had grabbed a camera from some reporter and had taken a picture of the words tenderly etched into the heartwood of each tree stump so many years ago, a picture of love and old-time sepia truth. That picture confirmed the rumor, the mythology, and it was worth more than a million words or a million pieces of silver.

The scrawny naked Digger guy stood directly in front of Thomas Goast, holding the camera.

Thomas Goast wanted that camera. He wanted that picture.

The Digger guy laughed.

Thomas Goast didn't laugh. "I want that picture!" Thomas Goast said.

The Digger guy laughed a scrawny laugh.

Then they grabbed him by his scrawny naked neck.

But he had thrown the camera to the Digger woman who looked like Lady Godiva. She was even faster than he, which didn't really surprise me. Liddy helped by blocking one of the police officers who tried to arrest Lady Godiva as she ran with the camera. What a woman! What a block!

I was happy as I watched the Digger woman run away. There was a picture, a bit of hope, one bit of truth. She had a photo of words etched in the rings of aged heartwood. She had a picture of their love for all to see.

That Digger guy simply laughed, and he didn't seem to care that he had been nabbed. He didn't care about being naked or having wire-rimmed glasses. He just laughed and said something about planting seeds. He just said power was always inside. Power never wore clothes. He said the power was inside those trees, like the germ inside of every seed. The words were inside. Songs were inside. He said eternity was inside.

That's what he said.

He knew about the power inside the human heart, an immense space like the sacred soil from which Noah and Eloise were nourished. That's what he said to us. Then they cuffed him and took him off to jail. I will always remember the Digger's laugh as they took him away. It was a different laugh from my

150

own at Squeegee's hearing. I laughed to avoid the urge to vomit. This was a lovely laugh, a laugh flowing with purity—like the Euphrates River on the fourth day of creation.

Thomas Goast stood watching all of this. There weren't many people still in the area. The Druids had been arrested. Henry Thumm had been cuffed with them. The Hare Krishna sect was occupying a consciousness and existence far removed from the grass on which they chanted, so the police were hard pressed to arrest them for trespassing. Only a few city workers remained, probably out of some loyalty to their paychecks. Liddy and Franklin were arguing. Well, Liddy was shouting into Franklin's face because the guy had, in the commotion, stepped on Moses, the new oak she had so recently planted.

Boy! Could that woman yell!

Thomas Goast looked straight at me. Then he butchered any trace of Noah's trunk. Eloise was next. The bits of both stumps that remained hardly resembled wood. They looked more like the remnants of Dresden after a big bombing raid. There would be no more pictures for anyone to examine.

Finally, he allowed the chainsaw to sputter to silence. "There are your trees. Now," he said loudly. "Who's next? How about that sick one? What's her name, Erna? Let's put her out of her damn misery!"

Thankfully, one of our local police officers approached him. As the cop turned toward me, I recognized him as Officer Tim Paine, a good guy. He would be, in time, the police officer who would be shot to death while on routine nighttime patrol, and it was during his funeral the rabble would sing "I Shot the Sheriff." This lovely man tried to reason with Thomas Goast. They talked, and Officer Paine put his arm around Thomas Goast. I think Officer Paine had to produce his badge, and perhaps he threatened to arrest him. I don't know. I saw Thomas Goast say something. From a short distance I thought I saw him mouth the words, "Whatever you say." However, he might have said, "I'll make you pay." Who knows? Take your choice. Whatever Officer Paine suggested seemed to work.

Erna and the others would be saved for yet another day.

I waited for Liddy. She had tried her best to set the little Moses tree upright again. As I watched her tuck the tiny tree back into the ground, I felt a soft hand on my arm. I turned to find Elvis and Uncle Ho standing there in the rain. Uncle Ho smiled and nodded his head. He was returning the favor for my comments at his grandson's murder hearing. I wanted people to protest, so he was here to protest. Uncle Ho said something to Elvis.

"My grandfather," Elvis translated, "says he watches your government. He says he watches and he learns everything."

I thanked them both for coming and standing in the rain.

Uncle Ho spoke a bit more to Elvis. "My grandfather is happy so many people showed up today. He says not enough people care about what your government does. In his old country, to know too much is bad. They shut you up. They kill you. That's what they do."

"Thank you," I said. I couldn't think of anything else to say. It was a very American thing to say.

"My grandfather goes to every meeting. He hears everything. He hears everything that is not said. He knows all about these people who are your government."

I simply said, "Thanks" again.

"My grandfather wants to tell you something he knows. It's very important."

I listened intently.

"He says those people are afraid you will find that dog."

"What dog?"

"The dog they took."

"Dara?"

Uncle Ho smiled and shook his finger. He was excited as Elvis explained what he knew. "My grandfather says you must find the dog. Those people who want to cut the trees don't want you to find that dog."

"Why not?" I asked.

"Because," Elvis said, "because my grandfather wants to tell you there is a puppy." I was excited. Uncle Ho continued to gesture with his finger.

"How does he know?" I asked.

"My grandfather listens to every one of those people. He hears what they say. He hears what they do not say. He knows. He knows there is puppy."

His word was good enough for me. His word was a debt for which I could find no recompense. I could only trust him. That was the best I could do. Perhaps it's the best thing anyone can do in an attempt to offer a bit of thanks. Even after all these years, all I can say is the word of this old man, Uncle Ho, was as great as any song by The Clash.

Uncle Ho told me we should all stay forever free.

What an incredibly wonderful thing to say, whether it is spoken in Vietnamese or whispered in English without a trace of an accent.

a Picture and a Possible Puppy

SO THERE WAS A PICTURE, a picture of the words Noah had written long ago to his Eloise on that old oak tree. That picture made the front page of our *Green Bay Press-Gazette*. The headline read, "Tree Reveals Message in Its Rings!" I suppose it did. Well, sort of, because it was really difficult to tell from the photo.

Some people clearly saw the words "My Dearest Eloise" etched in the heartwood of the tree formally known as Noah, so it should have been easy for the mythology of the trees to be true. I wanted it to be true. It was such a beautiful truth to know. Somebody else saw the face of Jesus. Somebody always sees the face of Jesus. Somebody else saw nothing at all.

Hank Nitze, a cook at Kroll's East—the best hamburger place in town—claimed he saw the Green Bay Packer emblem in the rings of the old wood. Everyone was suddenly excited—in lottery euphoria. The Packer season was about to start with a home game against the Chicago Bears—our archenemy—and the guy who cooked the best burgers in town suggested the Green Bay Packer emblem was seen in the contours of these old oak's rings. This was a Green Bay Packer miracle, a National Football

A PICTURE AND A POSSIBLE PUPPY

League miracle, a Sunday in September miracle, and a Heaven-be-praised miracle! The smell of holy bratwurst was in the air! Saint Vince was praised!

The excitement grew. Gladys Hooper, a bartender at BB's Bar and amateur wrestler of some local renown, claimed to have poured a beer from the tap only to see the beer bubbles rise and form a near-perfect replica of the famous Lombardi Superbowl Championship Trophy. Sadly, Gladys was unable to photograph the miraculous trophy, but her story made front-page speculation in the local paper.

There was more: At Chili John's chili restaurant, a kid named Andy Pizer found a chili bean having marks resembling the lacings on an actual NFL football. That bean, I do believe, is still on display at the restaurant, even to this day.

Amid all the excitement, my trees became celebrities. Everyone wanted to know about Erna and her stuffed dog; and with equal interest, they wanted to know about Peter and Paul, who were deemed heroes and saints. That was good. Thomas Goast backed off from his threats. An amazing number of people bought trees and planted them in their yards, and an equally amazing number of girl babies were suddenly christened with the names Erna and Eloise. There was even a Thecla or two. *People* magazine sent a reporter to investigate our story. We actually made page thirty with a small story without a picture.

A few preachers came to town and began to sermonize about divine football intervention. Politicians wanted their pictures taken with little kids in Packer attire, and the local bishop did his duty, too. He saw the Packer emblem in the photo and decided to use the picture in his televised Sunday mass sermon before the Green Bay Packer season opener against the much-hated Chicago Bears. Hallelujah! Hallelujah in green and gold!

So, he prayed over the picture taken by the skinny naked Digger guy. He prayed over the picture of the tree that, heaven only knows, said various things to all sorts of people. The bishop prayed anyway, and boy, did those prayers deliver their miracle. This was no mere miracle of divine healing — no leper was made clean; no blind man was made to suddenly see; no demon was cast out of an unfortunate soul; no sea, whether it was red, green, black, or sliver, was parted. This miracle was much greater than that. This was a Packer victory miracle over those much-hated Chicago Bears!

I went to the big game. I saw the miracle and witnessed the magic. It's hard to understand, but Green Bay Packer tickets were easy to find. Now they are solid gold without the green, but nobody wanted to go to the games in 1980. That's the way it was back then. But I went. The tickets were free. I found the two twenty-yard-line tickets tucked under my windshield wiper blade on Sunday morning. I think it was some sort of joke. So, Liddy and I went together to see our Packers play those Monsters of the Midway — our archfiends, the much-hated Chicago Bears. I may have held Liddy's hand as we went through the turnstile of Lambeau Field. I really don't remember. All I know is we were at a Packer game together, which was enough for any true-blooded Green Bay Packer fan. Not only that, but it was almost a real date.

The date was September 7, 1980, a Sunday. Of course it was a Sunday. God rested on Sunday because he knew someday, after the rise and fall of countless civilizations, there would finally be professional football to watch. God is a patient guy, and Packer football on a Sunday is worth the wait. An

A PICTURE AND A POSSIBLE PUPPY

autumnal breeze carried the smell of bratwurst cooking on tailgate grills. Packer fever was fervid. The picture of Noah, or at least what was left of old Noah, had graced the front page of the sports section in the *Green Bay Press-Gazette*. The photo was blurry, and some people still saw the face of Jesus, while others saw words of eternal love. But let's face the facts: This was Green Bay, and everybody saw the Packer emblem — the omen of good so desperately desired for the season opener at Lambeau Field.

Boy, were the goods delivered. God does, indeed, work in wondrous and mysterious ways. Our Packers had a fan-favorite kicker named Chester Marcol, who was a lovable character. We called him the Polish Prince. My grandfather was Polish, so I loved him. The entire city suddenly had a Polish relative, so the entire city loved Chester. These were the lean years. We all need a hero from time to time, and on that day in September, Chester was indeed our Polish Prince, our Polish hero.

With time fading quickly into the record books of this big-time rivalry, our Packers were tied with those much-hated Chicago Bears. Granted, a tie for the 1980 Packer team was oddly equivalent to say, successfully landing men on Mars, but still the fans' fever pitch demanded much more. The fans wanted the blood of victory. And so it came to pass: We all felt each painful second tick as Lynn Dickey, a true saint of a Packer quarterback, threw a pass to wide receiver James Lofton. The stage was certainly set for a thirty-four-yard field goal that would appease the attending moms, dads, kids, and everyone else who watched or listened to Jim Irwin's Packer play-by-play commentary. The smell of bratwurst, like some strange incense at a religious ceremony, permeated the entire stadium.

I held Liddy's hand.

THE GOSPEL ACCORDING TO DARA

Then Chester Marcol, our Polish Prince, kicked the ball. Liddy's hand crushed my fingers. Even from my sarcastic view of life, this field goal, for a moment, meant everything. I winced because I was in pain, but I opened my eyes to see that football strike the face mask on the helmet of Alan Page, the big Chicago defensive lineman. The crowd groaned in disbelief!

I groaned!

Liddy screamed! Her hand squeezed mine so tightly I felt one finger bone snap out of its proper place!

The football bounced upward, into the rarified bratwurst air of Lambeau Field. And we all watched, without the possibility of a breath, as Chester Marcol caught the football in mid-stride and ran as only an NFL kicker could run, into the left side of the end zone.

We won! God is a Packer fan!

Liddy hugged me! This was almost like a real date!

I hugged her back. It was almost a real hug. Noah and Eloise were gone; Otis was gone; Moses was dead; and sure, Ronald Reagan was about to be elected President of the United States, but in that moment, we overcame all of that. We didn't move beyond the bad stuff; rather, we found a way into it. Some may say it's just the eye of the storm. I think it's much deeper than that.

There is a mythological Celtic belief that there is a space between the bark and the tree. They believe divine spirits live there, and deities exist in the spaces between all things. Our Packer football moment was something like that: It was a place between all others things — other things in the NFL that stood for big business and profit. The Packers are a breath of fresh air in professional football. Packer cheerleaders don't look like checks demanding to be cashed. I think Mrs. Fletcher knew about that space. That's why she taught music. That's why she loved words. That's why she loved dogs and trees. That's why the rest of those old oaks should always exist. Those trees are a space, a pause, a breath, a drink of fresh water, a Packer victory, perhaps even a deity, found within the machinations of our busy bustle—the sad building blocks of Babel, the building blocks we use to erect the exact image—the likeness of a God—we so desperately wish to be.

Amen.

Amen again, because our Packers won; and in Green Bay on a Sunday in September, that's all that really matters.

Of course, I needed to talk to Jenny Ego, the owner of Dara Ruthie Rose. If there really were a puppy, then Franklin could not cut down the rest of the beautiful trees, according to Mrs. Fletcher's will. It stated the trees could not be cut until old Otis and any of his descendants were dead. Well, if there were a puppy, a descendent of Otis, that puppy could save us all.

Jenny Egolenski, amazingly, was in the phone book. It was all too easy. Not only was she listed in the residential white pages, but she also had a yellow pages ad. She offered song lyrics for sale, but her ad went well beyond that. Her services had grown to include "short stories, poems for any occasion," and something she called "fiction-based research papers."

Apparently, she had taken her many short story ideas and converted them into so-called research based on imaginary ideas. At first, I thought the two were somehow incompatible. Fiction is fiction, and fact is fact. Now I'm really not so certain. America waged war in Vietnam for too many years because of an attack in the Gulf of Tonkin that never really happened. About forty years later, America attacked Iraq based on supposed facts about weapons of mass destruction that apparently were about as authentic as the attack on the *USS Maddox* that sucked our country into the Vietnam quagmire. Ronald Reagan, who was soon to be elected president, was the master at blending movie trivia with authenticity. So who am I to suggest countless thousands of young American minds in High School, USA, should tell the truth? Jenny's fiction-based research was, in golfing lingo, par for the course on which American politicians often played.

I dialed the number, held my breath, and thought about the remaining oak trees. I heard a voice say, "Hello, this is Jenny Ego of Jenny Ego, Ltd., your source for all your creative-writing needs. We have a special this week. For no extra cost with the purchase of a short story or poem for any occasion, we will include the name of somebody you dislike as the moniker for an evil person in that story or poem."

That's not a bad idea, I thought. Then I mentally cataloged all the names of people I didn't like very much.

Several seconds passed because my list was fairly long.

"Hello?" Jenny's voice said.

"Jenny Egolenski?" I asked.

"I'm sorry," the voice said. "She only exists in an edition of this book that is sadly no longer in print."

"I must have the wrong number."

"Oh no," she said. "You have the correct number. It's just that she is out of print at the current moment."

I was a bit confused.

"But don't worry," the voice explained. "She'll be reissued. Everything is always reissued."

"So who are you?"

A PICTURE AND A POSSIBLE PUPPY

"This is Jenny Ego. Not Egolenski. You can talk to me if you want. I'm always here."

I suddenly understood. I had fallen into the web of Jenny's imagination. She refused to throw the baby, the washtub, or the bath water out. She saved everything, and she expected everybody to understand her world. We humans have fallen for so many things, like Satan's sales pitch, chemically treated lawns, and the internal-combustion engine, to name just a few. Jenny's imagination wasn't the worst thing.

"All right," I said. "I really need to talk to you."

"I really need to talk to you," she said.

"Why?"

"Because I have a few questions."

"Questions?"

"Yes, questions." Jenny paused for a moment. "Do you think..." she started to ask. "Do you think if we contact aliens who had a third ear..." she paused again. "Do you think those aliens with three ears would have a Q-Tip with a third prong?"

I was stumped. "I suppose so." I had never thought about that. I didn't even know that I was supposed to think about those things. The problem with Jenny was that she controlled every situation. Jenny left me with the feeling I was a character in a short story she was writing. Her imagination was really strong.

"May I use your name?" she asked. "If I can use your name, then I will include you in my fiction-based research paper."

"I guess you can." I had never been quoted in a research paper. I felt important.

"By the way, who are you?" she asked. "May I quote your comment in my research paper?"

"I hope you remember me. I'm Joshua Toss. I wrote that song called 'White Gold.' Everyone remembers that song. It's not about cocaine. It's about smuggling oleomargarine from Michigan back to Wisconsin."

There was a heavy silence. "No," she said. "Sorry. I don't remember your song. Was it famous?"

I didn't know what to say. I had never met someone who didn't know that stupid song. "It doesn't matter," I said.

"But I remember you," she said.

"You do?"

"Sure. You're the sarcastic guy."

"That's one way of looking at it," I said.

"Looking at what?"

"Sarcasm."

She paused. "So you are the sarcastic guy?"

"Sure."

"All right, sarcastic guy, may I ask a sarcastic question?"

What could I say?

"If you make a sarcastic comment about another sarcastic comment, does that make it a compliment?"

I thought about her idea. It was similar to the negative-number subtraction conversation Liddy and I had some time ago. "Why do you ask?" I said.

"It's all research," she said.

I felt like I was either praying or asking the Ouija board some weird question. Jenny's imagination was so strong.

"So what do you want to know?" she asked again.

"I want to know about Dara."

"Dara, the dog?"

"Yes," I said this with a strange form of reverence.

"Well, she's gone."

"Where?"

"I don't know."

A PICTURE AND A POSSIBLE PUPPY

For crying out loud! How could she not know? She knew about aliens with three ears and weird Q-Tips!

"She's just gone," Jenny said.

"Gone?"

"And her puppy."

"Her puppy?"

"She was stolen. I don't know. Somebody took her. They took her and her puppy."

"When?"

"I don't know. They're just gone."

"I need them. I need Dara and her puppy to save the rest of the old oak trees."

"I'm sorry," she said. "They're just gone, vanished."

I had expected more.

Here was a woman who seemed to create life as she talked. Much later in life, of course, I would be given a garden rake during the final moments of Mr. Raymond's Big Bang Sale. I would then understand Jenny's answer. She controlled by giving everything away. That's how she created, but during that phone conversation, I was merely frustrated. What could I say? Dara and her puppy were gone. They had disappeared.

Then she said, "We should try to get them back."

"We?"

"Sure," Jenny explained. "We can figure all this out. I want my Dara back. You know her name means wisdom and compassion in Gaelic, don't you?"

I didn't know that. But truly, it was a great name for an Irish setter. Jenny talked on and on. The woman was simply full of stories. She talked in bits and pieces, but somehow, it all made sense, even though her stories always chased their tails. Everything circulated like oxygen-rich blood in the veins of her words. "Trust me," she said. "Everything always works out just fine."

I didn't say anything. But believe me—I distinctly heard a character in one of Jenny Ego's stories say, "Well, that's one way of looking at it."

a Fiction-Based Apocalypse

"I WONDER WHO PICKS OUT THE ARTWORK to hang in places like this," Jenny Ego said. I looked about me at the walls of the Big Boy restaurant in which we met to discuss strategy. It wasn't a pretty sight. "I'd like to know if this stuff was chosen because somebody important thinks it's good, or if the whole selection process is just a bad joke. You know: 'Let's see how much stupidity we can get away with before someone understands they are the butt of a bad art joke.'"

"But," Liddy suggested, "this place isn't about art. It's about food."

"America's about food," Henry Thumm interjected.

"No," I said, "America's about money."

Uncle Ho said nothing.

Elvis just examined the menu.

"Hotels are the same thing," Jenny said.

"What do you mean?" I asked.

"The art. I wonder whose job it is to select the decor."

"Hotels aren't about art," Liddy said. "They're about cheap comfort."

"America's about cheap comfort," Henry Thumm interjected, again.

A FICTION-BASED APOCALYPSE

Uncle Ho said nothing.

It was great to have Jenny back. As I have said, Jenny Ego made me feel she was some sort of creator because her mind was always electric with activity. I wanted to be part of that electricity. If nothing else, she could write a story about trees and dogs. The imagination is pretty strong. For William Blake, the English poet who invented punk rock in the eighteenth century, the imagination was reality, and I was ready. As far as I was concerned, Jenny's return was as good as any other apocalyptic tale. Existing in someone else's fiction is just another name for a good game of dodge ball with reality. We all like to dodge reality because reality is tough stuff to swallow. So we solve mathematical equations to avoid it, and we even like to believe there is, perhaps, a germ of truth in the stories in which we exist: The Gospel of Jenny Ego, The Gospel of Otis, The Gospel of Dara, The Gospel of Mrs. Fletcher, The Gospel of Some Naked Digger Guy. The list could go on and on. It may even include the Gospel of Thomas Goast. I was just happy because in any version of the truth, I was always allowed to be sarcastic.

Elvis just continued to examine the menu.

"That's the point of everything?" Jenny Ego asked.

"What's the point of everything?" I asked, lost in her idea.

"To give in."

"What do you mean?" I asked again.

"Saying yes when the answer is obviously no," she said.

Elvis continued to examine the menu.

She continued, "Or saying no when the answer is obviously yes."

I was definitely confused.

So she continued to explain, "We all do what we are told to do."

I examined the menu, which is what I always did in a

restaurant, what everybody does in a restaurant. The Big Boy Double Burger appealed to me. The bun had sesame seeds on it.

"Watch," Jenny said. "The waitress will say something that she knows isn't funny at all, but she will laugh."

"Why would she do that?" I asked.

"That's her job."

"To pretend to laugh?"

"No. Her job is to play the game."

"What game?" I asked.

"The same game we will all play by laughing at her joke."

"Why will we do that?"

"Well," Jenny said, "it's better than locking the door to your music store, or your shoe store, or bookstore, or perhaps even your hardware store for the final time because some big chain has cut your throat with offers of mega-savings and even bigger shopping carts." Jenny paused and then added, "So we all laugh at bad jokes. We say yes when we want to say no. What else can we do? If we don't play the game, there is always a price to be paid. And believe me, it's always more than the cost of a fast-food cheeseburger."

I was still thinking about the sesame seeds on that bun. I would not, of course, really understand Jenny's comments until much later when I stood with a gallon of melting ice cream in my hands and watched Mr. Raymond lock his door for the final time.

I suddenly wanted to ask God about calories — the calories in a double cheeseburger with sesame seeds on the bun. Perhaps the calorie count should be in proportion to the food's weight. That way, the amount of effort needed to lug the junk food around — and digest the stuff — might burn away the ingested calories. My double cheeseburger should weigh 175 pounds. A

A FICTION-BASED APOCALYPSE

fast food restaurant would be the same as—say—an all purpose gymnasium. Customers who braved deep-fried cheese curds would be required to don the support belts worn by those heavy-duty hairy Russians who lift those big weights for Olympic gold medals.

I suddenly thought about Tommy Carvaka—a friend of mine who just happened to be a Jainist. He believed that any interaction with the living world—and eating a double cheeseburger certainly constituted interaction with the living world—resulted in karma burden, the stuff that clings to your jiva and causes endless births and deaths that prevent an ultimate spiritual release—a release all Jainists, including my friend Tommy Carvaka, so desperately desire.

I looked at my cheeseburger and wanted to ask the waitress how many lifetimes I would have to relive in the endless karma cycle for a taste of Big Boy's finest burger and a serving of fries.

But I never asked.

Instead, I simply laughed at her joke—a joke that really wasn't funny. Perhaps that laugh is the true source of karma burden.

Jenny was Jenny—the writer of many rock band lyrics. She suddenly paused. Jenny noticed Elvis' American history textbook, the one called *America: The Land and Its Promise*, the one his grandfather, Uncle Ho, forced him to tote around and read. "It starts there," she said.

"In that history book?"

"No, in school. That's where we are all taught to say 'yes' when we desperately want to say 'no.'"

"Or we say 'no' when we all want to sample the forbidden fruit," Liddy added.

"Please," I said, "don't talk about drugs."

THE GOSPEL ACCORDING TO DARA

"Drugs?" Jenny asked.

"Yeah, you know, white gold, the forbidden fruit." I paused to emphasize my point. "You know," I slowly enunciated the word, the bane of my life, as I said, "oleomargarine." Jenny shook her head and spoke with a haunted voice that belied the sarcasm of the rock 'n' roll lyrics about a Crouton invasion she had written for the band with so many names. She simply said, "We should laugh with our tears. Schools should teach that. We don't want the tears. So we're taught to laugh without the pain. That's just clever graffiti written without a drop of blood in the spray can. We should cry right out loud, and we should cry every day because the gods to whom we pray can never bleed paint onto the marble walls of their own shrines. They know that. They're not dumb. But we are—we laugh with the hollow echo of a Las Vegas casino slot machine because, well, we have lost the will to weep."

She paused.

I think the entire Big Boy restaurant paused.

Then she said, "The forbidden fruit has nothing to do with any drug. Tears will unlock the gates of servitude. Blood will make us weep with wise compassion. Eve didn't eat anything. She had an idea. She wept while shaking hands with her own death. Her son's tears would, indeed, punctuate her final breath. That's why she was dangerous. She bled. The gods condemned her for singing songs—sad songs, happy songs, sweet songs, nasty songs—tunes disappearing into the very breath of which they were born. The gods listened in envy because these tunes were the only thing in the universe beyond their comprehension. Then they made us invent religion, so we would think death somehow ceased to exist. Religion is simply an attempt to censure all the lovely music escaping from Eden."

A FICTION-BASED APOCALYPSE

I said nothing, nothing at all. What could I say? This was the very same woman who had written about Croutons and their Earth takeover bid. She had just spoken the words of my autobiography, a story I didn't have the guts to write myself.

Uncle Ho glanced at me with very hard and sad eyes. I felt the urge for a slice of apple pie without a piece of cheese.

The waitress came, gave us all a glass of water, and said something.

We all laughed.

I glanced at Henry Thumm, our practicing Greek Mythologist. He loved the intricacies of Greek mythology, and he once explained to me while we ate ice cream that life and religion are like some great tapestry that begs close examination, one lovely thread at a time.

I was at the school board meeting as Henry pleaded his case for his Greek mythology to be taught in the science curriculum at the school he attended in the district. He only asked for a small amount of class time and a moment of respect. Several of the school board members, however, fought to hold back their laughter. One didn't even bother. Apparently, they had had enough of this frivolity. Earlier in the meeting, two other people had requested the high school offer a music class allowing kids to play rock music and get credit just like anybody else who played in a jazz band or symphony orchestra.

I knew both of the rock 'n' roll advocates. One was an odd guy everyone knew as Rock 'n' Roll Randy. Randy spoke in rock 'n' rollese, the linguistic equivalent of a really cool record collection. The other was a local musician, Mr. U., who probably played in every band that ever graced a local stage. He'd been a member of A Warped Window?—the band that gave me my fifteen minutes of celebrity status. He was our drummer long enough to get fired because he wanted to rock while the others wanted only to venture into the vast vacuity of space that, at least to my ears, sounded a lot like the low hum of a refrigerator.

"Eddie and the Hotrods," Rock 'n' Roll Randy said to the school board. "'Don't Believe Your Eyes,'" he continued. "'Making Plans for Nigel,' 'No Surrender,' 'Jungleland,' John Fogerty, Rikki Nadir, The Sound, Wire, *Pink Flag*, 'Mr. Suit,' you know. *Chairs Missing*." Randy was seriously trying to plead his rock 'n' roll case. So he spoke in the language of his heart. "'Radio, Radio,' Pink Floyd. 'Another Brick in the Wall,' Richard Thompson. *Henry the Human Fly*, The Kinks, you know, 'Here Come the People in Grey,'" he said.

Mr. U. simply said, "Isn't it about time kids in school got to say 'yes'—when they really wanted to say 'yes?'" The school-board members smiled plastic inert smiles. Mr. U., who had brought his drumsticks to the meeting, tried to explain. He said school should be about excitement and passion, rather than offering numbing injections of knowledge that managed to kill just enough time to make it to the final bell.

Mr. U. had, incidentally, been in a band called The Numbing Injections of Knowledge. After that, he formed a rock 'n' roll power trio called Three Wise Men. The band took the stage names of Gaspar, Balthasar, and Melchior. Mr. U. was Gaspar and had to dress in silly robes and a turban. They cut a good single called "Rockin' in the Manger." The flipside was a cover of the ever-popular Teardrop Explodes song "Window Shopping for a New Crown of Thorns." The local born-again religious people filled every bar they played. A radio station DJ known only

as Doctor Revolution coined the term "Bible Rock." On the precipice of fame, the band released a second single. Unfortunately,
nobody in the band was a gifted songwriter, so they opted for
the next-best thing. They took two of their favorite rock 'n' roll
chestnuts and simply rewrote the lyrics. "Rock Around the
Clock" became "Rock Around the Cross," and Steppenwolf's
ode to "heavy metal thunder," "Born to Be Wild," morphed into
the perennial crowd favorite, "Born to Be Crucified."

Record companies smelled big bucks.

Then Mr. U., the engine room of the band's heavy sound,
suddenly quit. He simply said he couldn't drum with the robes
and turban. So he turned his back on Bible Rock stardom.

Recently, I found a copy of Three Wise Men's first single,
"Rockin' in the Manger," in a collector's store. I bought it for three
dollars. I asked the record-store guy about that second single.
The guy just shook his head. "You find that record," he said, "and
I'll give you a blank check." He said, "'Rock Around the Cross'
was a great song, but 'Born to be Crucified' was" — and these are
his words — "the magical elixir of rock 'n' roll." He told me the
song could cure the blind and make the obsessive-compulsive
person lose the will for perfection. I suppose this was no different from the gold, frankincense, and myrrh brought to the baby
Jesus by the original three wise men. Even after all these years,
I still search for a copy of that record. That record is a bit like
the Holy Grail.

So by the time Henry Thumm attempted to discuss his
concerns about Greek mythology, the school board had lost its
patience. The plastic smiles were gone. The board members didn't
even bother to vote on Henry's issue, which would, at least, have
been a polite façade. Elected people in America should always
have the decency to present a polite façade.

THE GOSPEL ACCORDING TO DARA

I stopped Mr. U. and Rock 'n' Roll Randy after the meeting and told them I really liked Greek mythology and rock music. They both appreciated my concern. Ironically, Mr. U. would later play in a band called The Polite Façade. I saw his band many times on the local bar circuit. They wrote a few very good songs but never managed to make any records, which was too bad.

Undeterred, Henry became the advocate of all seemingly useless causes. He was, of course, arrested with the Druid people who protested the cutting of Noah and Eloise, even though he had never visited Stonehenge. That was the reason he joined us at the local Big Boy restaurant to discuss our possible rebellion against Crouton people everywhere—Crouton people who want to pray the mantra of a chainsaw rosary on bended knee to the profit prophets singing the hosannas of miraculous stockmarket yields and sacred tax breaks.

Eventually, everyone at the table met one another. We were an odd group. Jenny, of course, was our resident creator, with a need to find her Dara, the Irish setter whose name meant "wisdom" and "compassion" in ancient Gaelic. Henry Thumm was the practicing Greek Mythologist who worshipped trees and had a soft spot in his heart for almost any cause, simply because he knew what it was like to be tossed aside like some country without an oil deposit tucked within the bowels of its borders. Uncle Ho and Elvis were both refugees from war-torn Vietnam. They attended every local city meeting. They watched and listened to everything that was said and not said. Liddy was always Liddy. Yes, we were certainly an odd group.

"The problem is," I suggested, "they were going to leave the other trees alone after the Packers won, but now Thomas Goast is suggesting we should cut down one tree before each game as some sort of sacrifice."

A FICTION-BASED APOCALYPSE

Henry Thumm looked worried. As a practicing Greek Mythologist, he worshipped the deities who lived in those trees. "America is always about sacrifice," he said. "I just don't want those trees to be the poster children for the American dream."

"If we can find my Dara and her puppy," Jenny Ego said, "then the trees will be all right. We have to find Dara."

Uncle Ho said nothing.

Elvis still examined the menu.

The waitress eventually took our order.

Jenny Ego asked for a salad, but she insisted it be served without croutons. Apparently, she didn't want to start an intergalactic incident.

I followed suit and ordered a bowl of soup, but I refused soup crackers. Sure, it sounds foolish now, but at the time, I thought, perhaps, in some scheme of the universe, there might be alien Soup Cracker creatures who would take offense at the idea of being consumed by somebody on planet Earth.

It was then I saw Henry Thumm's eyes light up, like an airport runway at night. I followed his gaze and saw, as she sat in the booth across from ours, Ms. Helen Turnkee, the English teacher who had quietly moved the study of Greek mythology into her nonfiction unit, despite the school board's refusal to honor Henry's request. We all loved her, and we all knew her. She was our Ms. Turnkee, our Helen, who came from Sparta, Wisconsin, to teach us in Green Bay. We felt somehow sadly diminished when we heard she was not returning to teach in our school. There were only rumors: She quit. She was fired. We just didn't know. All we knew was she was not coming back. She sat alone at her table. Henry's eyes found her glance. She was that kind of teacher. Henry turned red and suddenly forgot how to take a breath.

"Well, hello, Mr. Thumm," she said.

Henry turned a shade of red yet to be invented by Crayola.

"What brings you here?" she asked.

Henry managed only three words: "Dogs and trees."

Jenny explained, "We're here to find my Dara. She's an Irish setter whose name means 'wisdom' and 'compassion.' Somebody stole her. They took Dara and her puppy."

"Where have you looked?" Ms. Turnkee asked.

Nobody said anything.

"I see. Well," Ms. Turnkee said, "if I were searching for a dog like your Dara, let's see." She paused in thought. "Let's see, where would I go?"

"To the Oracle at Delphi?" Henry offered hopefully.

"Well, Mr. Thumm," she said, "that would be the second place I would look."

Henry beamed a second-place smile.

"The very first place I would look before I traveled all the way to Delphi would be a place much closer to home."

Elvis put his cheeseburger down.

"Yes," Ms. Turnkee said, "I know. If you want to find out about bad people and dogs, there's only one place to look."

Elvis took an indifferent bite of his cheeseburger.

Then she said, "The mall."

"Is there a dog show?" Liddy asked.

"Oh no. But there's a pet store. Every mall has a pet store. Just about every mall gets its puppies from puppy mills. That's where you want to look. Go to the mall. Find out where they get their dogs."

Well, we certainly didn't have a better idea. She was Ms. Turnkee, a favorite teacher who had quietly added the study of Greek mythology to her nonfiction unit despite the school board forbidding any such action. So that was our plan. It was all we had, but at least it was something.

Elvis finished his cheeseburger and fries. The kid had a good appetite. I thought about my own father, the first generation of his family, born in America. His father, like Elvis, had emigrated here, too. My grandfather had tried sincerely to understand this new world, this opportunity called "America." I wondered what my grandfather thought as he watched his child, my father, lose the old world, with its dead-end poverty, its feudal system hand-me-downs, its potatoes, and, sadly, its beautiful Polish folk melodies. My grandfather had played the violin, not Stravinsky—Polish music—the music of the Polish ear, music of the Polish fields, and music of Polish dancing feet; he played the music of the Polish heart. Elvis finished his very last French fry. I wondered how my grandfather felt as he realized my father would never breathe the beauty of those Polish folk melodies. Sure, my father would know the Statue of Liberty and be able to read and write the English language. He would even recite the beginning of our Constitution. My dad played baseball well. But my grandfather knew my dad would never experience the laughter and the sorrow of Polish farm workers. That was finished.

Jesus said, "It is finished." It was over. Those are the saddest words ever spoken.

Polish people are intensely Catholic, so they all would have known what Jesus said, and they would have loved his words. They also would have known the sadness of those words as they watched their sons pay ten cents at the local theater in the middle of the downtown in almost every American town to watch a movie that lionized American movie stars, American ideas, and American music—a music that was clever, brand new, and highly entertaining—but a music devoid of the lilting Polish farm melodies left far behind in the old world of my grandfather's fading memory.

I felt a sudden compulsion to know Elvis' real name. I wanted to hear Vietnamese music. I had never known Moses' real name. He was always Moses. Even when he was shot, he was just Moses. That was my stupidity, and I wanted to get it right this time because I wanted America to get it right this time. We had goofed in Vietnam. I just didn't want to goof again.

"What's your name?" I asked with the conviction of an American saint.

"I'm Elvis," he said.

"No," I asked again. "What's your real name?" I felt a surge of morality. "What's your Vietnamese name? I want to know your real Vietnamese name."

"That is my name," Elvis told me.

"No," I insisted. "What is your Vietnamese name?"

"I was given an English name," he said, "because my mother knew we were coming here. She knew we were coming to America, so she named me Elvis. She thought it was a famous name, a name with a blessing. She believed it was a good name. She wanted me to be ready for America."

I felt disappointed, like a hero without a dragon to slay—John Wayne without an Apache warrior to kill. Every American hero needs a dragon to slay and a woman to save.

Uncle Ho smiled. He knew everything.

I was an American, so I should be the one who knew everything. But I didn't know much at all. I certainly didn't know any Polish folk melodies. I didn't even know how my family's name had been abbreviated when it was documented in the paperwork of Ellis Island. So I said nothing, and I sang nothing, but I hoped in time that I might learn Uncle Ho's real name. I wanted to know Moses' real name. Perhaps I could know my own name. I secretly hoped to someday sing the same songs Polish field workers sang before they decided to come to this place called America.

an Extra-Large Victor Jara

I WOULD LOVE TO SAY there was a miraculous appearance that suddenly made everything all right. Even a character steeped in sarcasm like myself never quite sheds the final bastion of hope. Call me human. Sadly, nothing happened. The big downtown mall into which we ventured was a bit like ancient church attendees' idea of heaven. In 1980, the local mall was the epicenter of all things suburbia. The big fountain, of course, was an essential ingredient: We Americans are still searching for a mythical fountain of youth.

There were step dancers, or ballet dancers, or tap dancers; and every dancer smiled because, well, every dancer in a mall was required to smile. In a couple of years, a singer named Tiffany would use the mall forum to become famous and sell records. There were plants in the mall, and the air was climate-controlled. We could all shop in an endless cavalcade of chain stores. To many minds, it was a return to Eden.

Recently, years after the events of this story, I walked through the local mall. Nothing much had changed. Some malls have gone the way of the old west's ghost towns because the malls weren't big enough or climate-controlled enough, or because an anchor store's CEO suddenly realized its profit margin wasn't enough to warrant its existence. Perhaps a mega chain store moved in and sold everything, eliminating the need to visit separate shops.

Some big malls survived, and, as I said, nothing much has changed from the American mall, circa 1980. I was hard-pressed to find a big pretzel until I realized the powers that be had relocated all the restaurants to one central eatery, now called the food court. That was a convenient idea.

I noticed Che Guevara's image was everywhere. T-shirts with his face silk-screened were sold in the T-shirt store; his image was on the hats in the hat store; I won't even mention the lunch boxes. Che Guevara, for those who don't know, was a Marxist revolutionary who wrote several books on the theory of guerrilla warfare and was eventually taken captive during a military operation sponsored by our own American CIA. He was then executed. Quite frankly, it was amazing to see his image everywhere in the mall. When I checked to see where all of this merchandise was made, it was surprising to read the name of some country I couldn't even pronounce. I doubt those workers earned a living wage or could form a union to improve their working conditions. They just made T-shirts. What else could they do?

I asked the T-shirt salesman if he had anything in an extra-large Victor Jara, who wasn't a Marxist. He was a Socialist. Victor helped Salvador Allende get elected in Chile, and he sang songs of the common man, much like my grandfather played lovely Polish folk melodies on his violin. America backed a military coup in 1973 because our government didn't like the idea of a Socialist government in Chile. Victor Jara was brutally murdered while being held prisoner in a big stadium with other people who supported the Allende government. He was a revolutionary well deserving of a T-shirt, hat, poster, and lunch box, perhaps even a feature-length tearjerker movie from Hollywood.

Unfortunately, the salesman didn't know anything about Victor Jara. So I did what I was supposed to do: I said yes and bought a Che Guevara T-shirt. It was an extra-large—made in a country whose name I still could not pronounce. Then I went and washed my hands in the magnificent fountain in the mall. I stood next to a guy who wore a Cannibal Corpse T-shirt.

In 1980, any self-respecting mall had a pet store. All good dogs go to Heaven. Right. There were rumors. We all suspected the mall pet stores bought their dogs from puppy mills. But cute is cute. Profit is profit. No question asked is no question answered.

Lydia was already there. She wasn't Liddy. No, she was Lydia with at least one exclamation mark after her name. Boy! Could that woman get angry! She was really mad. Look up the word "truculent" in any dictionary. I stayed a safe distance from her foot. She told me everything. Believe me, everything was brutal—brutal beyond anything I expected to hear.

"Well," I said. "You should have waited for me. We could have pretended to be a couple looking for a puppy."

Boy! Was she mad!

"Then we could have asked questions," I suggested. "We could have asked about a basset–Irish setter mix. You shouldn't have yelled at the guy in the pet store. He's not going to help us now."

She kicked the mall bench. The bench made a rude sound.

AN EXTRA-LARGE VICTOR JARA

That was her response. Her blond dreadlocks punched at the stale mall climate-controlled air. It was like watching a news report and learning some astronaut's space suit had been punctured during a serious space walk to repair the Hubble telescope.

"I guess I can try," I said. "I can try to get some information from the pet store guy. I'll give him some money. He knows all about the puppy mills in the area. But you can't yell at him. I mean, what did you say to him?"

She told me.

I would need to up the ante of my bribe.

"Lydia," I said. "You have to calm down."

She said something about "Redemption Song" that any self-respecting dreadlock would know. Then she yelled some lyrics from a band called X-Ray Spex—a group I hadn't heard. I tried to reason with her. "I know all about punk music. Remember, I wrote those notebook entries. We need to be clever here. We have to get him to tell us what we want to know."

She kicked the mall bench again. The bench moved. I don't think it was designed to move. I took a chance and put my arm around her. She didn't kick me. We sat down on the mall bench—a bench still vibrating with her anger.

So there we were—vibrating together for a moment. Apparently, Lydia had confronted the pet store clerk, and, well, let's just say it was an ugly scene. Mall security had escorted her out of the store. That wasn't a good thing. I just wish she had waited for me. Of course, she wouldn't be Lydia, or even Liddy for that matter, if she had waited. What more could I ever expect? What more could I ever hope to expect? We sat there for a long time. Lydia cooled like the matter in the universe cooled after that big-bang explosion. If there is a God, believe me, he wants everything to cool down.

THE GOSPEL ACCORDING TO DARA

Lydia looked seriously at me, as if a few galaxies had congealed into a plan. I really did see the light bulb of an idea over her head. Of course, the light bulb was energy-efficient.

"Do you have any money?" she asked.

"Sure."

She took my wallet and was suddenly gone into the labyrinth of stores. I was left alone to watch American suburbia play itself out like a Charlie Chaplin film. The dancers danced in dance class, and there were the kids in a martial arts class. They broke things with their feet and hands, while parents applauded. I applauded but was thankful Lydia had not been given martial arts training. I felt the mall fountain spray. It was some distance away, but I still felt its spray. I watched as two people held hands and looked into a jewelry store window. He was too shy, and she knew he was too shy. I felt the spray of the big fountain again. Being shy is probably a good thing.

Some kid from the martial arts class broke another piece of wood. Good for him. Four girls giggled and walked into the arcade, which was called The Wizard. It had video games that cost twenty-five cents a play. In 1980, twenty-five cents allowed any gamester to defend our world from our Space Invader nemesis. I watched as a couple deliberated in the pet store. They didn't buy anything. They just looked, and they held hands as they looked. A puppy, I suppose, was a prelude to everything else in their future life. They held hands and walked through the mall. I hoped they would have a wonderful future.

Then a beautiful woman said, "What do you think?"

I replied, "About what?"

She said, "No. Stop joking. What do you think?"

I repeated, "About what?" I didn't know this woman.

Then she kicked me. I knew that kick, and I loved that kick.

AN EXTRA-LARGE VICTOR JARA

It was Lydia! She had high-heeled shoes, so the kick really hurt. My God! It was Liddy, but she wasn't the Liddy I knew. This was a Liddy with a short white skirt. This was a Liddy who had taken my money and bought all sorts of new clothes. This was a Liddy who had nylon stockings on her legs. I had never seen her real legs. Her knees had not seen the sun for at least ten years! This was a Liddy who had real legs with real knees and real ankles. Yikes! She had heels, real heels, and those high-heeled shoes looked nothing like her usual high-topped tennis shoes. Her arms were bare, too. I had never seen her arms so bare. Her arms had freckles, sexy freckles. Then I looked at her face. She had on make-up—making her a goddess right out of Henry Thumm's mythology. Her neckline was exposed. This was my Liddy with high heels and cleavage, and she had pulled her hair back to hide the dreadlocks. My God! This was my Liddy, whom I had known for an eternity.

Now she was sexy, absolutely sexy.

Liddy was absolutely beautiful.

But she had burnt bagel eyes.

"If you tell anybody about this," she threatened, "I will hurt you."

I forgot to take a breath.

My Lydia was back. "So you keep your mouth shut." That's all she said.

I have always liked my bagels fresh.

I couldn't shut my eyes—much less believe them. She was too different. She was no longer the woman who had rearranged the bones in my hand at a Packer game. Now she was the woman who had rearranged the bones in my hand at a Packer game and who wore a short skirt and looked sexy. I had to keep looking, and I had to watch her every moment. When guys are in love, we watch every movement of a woman. That's just the way it is. Adam, I imagine, looked at Eve's knees. He watched her ankles. She probably wore high heels. Eve's shoulders were probably pillow soft, like the fading image of the moon on a bright summer morning. That's why Adam ate the apple. It's hard to blame him. I would have taken a bite, too.

Of course, I couldn't say anything like that, but I certainly did my best to rise to the occasion. It occurred to me to say something to compliment her new clothes. I could have done that. Instead, I kept looking at her high-heeled shoes until I suddenly asked, "Can you run in those shoes?"

"Run?" she was confused.

"Yeah, what if a monster showed up right now in this mall, and I yelled, 'Run for your life!' What would you do? Could you run in those shoes? I always think about things like that. You never know when a monster might show up."

I should have been given a gold medal for immaturity.

The look on her made-up face told me she wasn't interested in a date if it meant sitting through a double feature of *It Came from Outer Space* and *The Creature from the Black Lagoon* while wearing 3-D specs. I felt stupid. I should have said something decent. Instead, I made up a joke about monsters. She didn't even bother to kick me. That hurt.

"Follow me. I have it all planned." That's all she said.

I really hoped her plan included yours truly as her boyfriend. Perhaps we were a couple. I hoped I starred in her plan as the man who held her hand.

I was wrong.

Liddy, with Swedish movie-star looks, walked in her high heels right up to the pet store guy who, apparently, had not responded to her threats.

AN EXTRA-LARGE VICTOR JARA

"May I help you?" the pet store guy said.

I could be wrong, but I swear Liddy pulled her shoulders back and introduced her cleavage in a more pronounced manner.

"Don't I know you? Weren't you just in here a while ago?" the poor guy said. "Didn't you yell at me?" He paused. "You're not going to yell at me again? Honest, I just work here because I have a car payment and my ex-girlfriend says she's pregnant. I don't even like dogs, and I hate ferrets. I mean, feeding the snakes is cool, but that's about it."

She didn't miss a beat. "Oh no," she explained. "That was my sister. I think she was here a little while ago."

"Your sister?"

"Yeah. I'm sure she was mean to you. She's a mean person. She probably threatened you. She always does that."

"She got mad and she shoved me," the poor guy said. "She started to scream about a dog she wanted to find."

Liddy shook her head. "Yeah. She is really mean. I'm sorry." I watched as she pulled her shoulders back a bit more. Yikes! "I apologize for my sister," she said sympathetically.

"That's all right," the pet store guy said. "How can I help you?"

"Well, no," she said. "I have two sisters. They are both really mean. Which one threatened you?"

"I don't know," he told her.

"Well," she said. "My friend here." She looked at me. "He's an exchange student from Yugoslavia. He doesn't speak English." She looked at me. "Isn't that right?"

"Sure," I said. "I don't speak English."

The pet shop guy didn't get the joke.

Then she shoved me. So much for holding hands!

"I don't speak English," I said, "but why did you do that?"

"That's the way one of my sisters shoves people." She thought for a moment. "That's Erna. She shoves people by pushing their shoulders. Did she push you like that?"

"I'm not sure," the pet store guy said.

Liddy was enjoying this way too much. Perhaps it was a payback for my monster question, but I had to be from Yugoslavia. I didn't know the Yugoslavian word for "ouch," so I didn't say anything.

Then she punched my chest, and I fell backward.

"That's Thecla," she said. "That's the way my sister Thecla punches people."

The mall pet store guy watched as I fell. I would like to think he felt sorry for me. "Could I see that again?" he asked. "I'm not sure." So much for sympathy— I felt like an optometrist, and the guy couldn't decide which lens he preferred. I got up, but Liddy shoved me again, twice. She was enjoying this way too much.

"Who found the glass slipper and decided you could be Cinderella?" I asked. I was from Yugoslavia, but that didn't stop the sarcasm.

"I think it was Erna," the pet store guy said.

"Erna. Erna." Liddy slowly shook her head. "I feel terrible. Is there anything I could do to make up for my sister's rude behavior? I'm really sorry. By the way," Liddy asked, "what did Erna want?" Liddy arched her back a bit more. Yikes again!

"She wanted to know about puppy mills and where we got our dogs."

"That's not much to ask," she said in a suddenly sexy voice.

"What do you mean?"

I was still on the mall floor. It was cold.

"I mean you could tell me about your dogs, couldn't you?" Her dress seemed to shrink before my very eyes!

AN EXTRA-LARGE VICTOR JARA

"Sure," the mall pet store guy said. "I could tell you all about our dogs." He paused. "I could tell you about where we get them. I know all kinds of stuff. The manager's an idiot. I practically run this place."

"That's what I want to know," Liddy said.

"That's what I will tell you."

"Well," Liddy said. She never looked more beautiful.

"Well," the mall pet store guy said. "I have tickets for a rock concert next Thursday night. I was trying to sell them." He pointed to a bulletin board. I saw his advertisement. There were all sorts of ads for various breeds of dogs. "How about it?" he asked. "I love REO and Styx."

"You mean a date?" Liddy asked with a hint of hesitation.

"Yeah. You and me." He paused, and then pointed his finger. He spoke really slowly so I could understand. "I only have two tickets." He waved two fingers toward my face. "That means Yugoslav here isn't coming with us." He slowed his speech even more. "Do you understand?" he said as he pointed his fingers at me.

I thought about my grandfather walking behind the police officer on his horse. My grandfather truly believed he was about to be shot. I felt like that. I wasn't ashamed of being from Yugoslavia; I wasn't even from Yugoslavia. I wasn't even ashamed of being an American. I was just really sad to realize this pet store assistant manager, this guy who had a car payment and an ex-girlfriend who said she was pregnant, this guy who was given so much, gave so very little concern for anybody else. He only cared about his car payment, sex, bad stadium rock music, and the snakes he liked to feed.

"Styx is playing with REO Speedwagon. It will be great!" he added.

THE GOSPEL ACCORDING TO DARA

Liddy, I should say, with or without her nylons and sexy white dress, normally wouldn't go to that concert for any money in the world. Those bands sang silly songs that were constantly played on the radio. I looked at her. I knew exactly what she was thinking: This pet store guy wanted her to like it when REO played "Take It On the Run." He wanted to hold her as Styx played "Lady," and he wanted her to hold a lighter in the air when Styx played some other silly Styx song. Liddy didn't smoke, so she didn't own a lighter to hold high in the air, but that was the proposition. It was a date. So take it or leave it.

She looked at me. I looked at her. I was still on the cold mall floor. Somehow, I managed to know her thoughts. Good friends can do this sort of thing. She had never been on a real date before, and her first real date should not include REO Speedwagon and being held by some pet store guy while Styx played "Lady" to idiots who liked that stupid song.

I said, "You're under the gun so take it on the run." It was yet another performance worthy of a gold medal for immaturity. That's what I said, but I hoped she could read my thoughts. I was really disappointed because I thought that Packer game, when she had snapped my finger bones out of their sockets, was a real date. I thought we planted the little Moses tree on a real date, but I was wrong. Those dates just didn't mean anything to her, and I felt my first real date should be with her, and I wanted her to feel the same way.

She looked at me.

The burnt bagels were gone.

I had never seen such tender eyes. These were omelet eyes—early morning eyes made with sunrise eggs. These eyes understood my heart. We knew each other's thoughts, and in that one glance, I felt every bone in my body snap and every joint rearrange and find a new dance partner. This was a very different type of pain. I knew what she was thinking, and she knew what I was thinking. There was only that glance, and that glance deciphered the hieroglyphic script of my every sarcastic comment. Liddy's problem was she cared too much. She somehow knew I cared about things, too.

"Of course," Liddy told the pet store guy whose ex-girlfriend said she was pregnant, "I'll go. I love..." She swallowed hard and looked at me. "I love REO Speedwagon. 'Take It on The Run.' Wow! And Styx! They sing 'Lady.' Sure. I'd love to go with you."

He smiled. He was happy. Of course he was happy. I mean, how many dates could a pet store guy like him get while working in a mall?

So when was I to tell her I knew where to find Dara? Sure. I figured it all out as Mr. Pet Store had pointed to the board with his tickets for sale. When should I tell her I knew everything? She had pushed me down four times, but that was all part of her plan to save the rest of the old oak trees. She was just playing a part. Sure. I suppose I should have told her, but I kept my mouth shut.

I watched as Liddy surrendered her telephone number—like a halfhearted striptease. I watched as she said good-bye. I watched her eyes. I knew exactly what she was thinking. I felt an intense sympathy for her situation. REO Speedwagon? Styx? A date with that guy? Holy cow!

So when was I to tell her?

You see, when the pet store guy pointed to the bulletin board to confirm his tickets for sale, I had scanned all the advertisements for any sign of Irish setters for sale. What else was there to do? Sure enough, one bit of paper read, "Irish setters! Any time—all the time!" I memorized the phone number and address by associating the numbers with prominent Green Bay Packer players. I always did that. Most people in Green Bay do that. What else did we have to do? So when was I to tell her? This was the place. I was certain. She didn't have to go on the date. She didn't have to be held in his arms as Styx sang "Lady."

"I guess I'll really have to go," she said slowly.

"Yeah," I said.

"Do you think I'll have to hold up a lighter and sway back and forth?"

"That's what they do at those concerts," I said.

"Do you think he'll expect another date?"

"Probably."

"What should I do? You're a guy. You should know."

"Yeah, well, I've never been on a real date." I was enjoying this too much. "But," I asked sincerely. "If I give you money, will you buy me a T-shirt? And try to get it autographed. Try to get both bands, and I want you to tape the concert. You should smuggle in one of those cassette recorders."

Then she knew. She shoved me hard. She was beautiful and wore high-heels, but she still shoved me really hard. "You know something, don't you?"

I told her everything. She brushed against me as she expressed her relief. I told her to just remember Bart Starr and Donny Anderson. That was the address, 1544. The street name was easy. The place was on Ellis Street. The Packer fullback was Gerry Ellis. I said that her street credibility as a punk rocker depended on her remembering those names.

As we left the mall, I noticed a bakery. A man and a woman were leaving, and the woman glanced at her sweet roll. I heard her say, "I know this is unbelievable, but look at the frosting. I mean, I know it's stupid, but, you know, don't the swirls in the frosting look like a face? Look at it. I've read about things like this. But this is really spooky. You know? Look at it."

The guy took the roll and carefully examined it. "You know," he said, "it looks just like the Virgin Mary. You know, just like the statues in the bathtubs." Then he took a bite of the sweet roll.

"So what should we do?" she asked.

He took another bite. That was his answer. In America, we eat first and ask questions later. He took a third bite, and then they continued to stroll down the endless American mall marketplace.

He didn't Think So — Twice!

"THE THING I LIKE ABOUT GREEK MYTHOLOGY," Henry Thumm said, "is they changed the story when they decided human sacrifice wasn't necessarily a good thing. They just changed the story."

"What do you mean?" Elvis asked. Uncle Ho looked at the stars in the September sky. Jenny Ego watched us all like a camera. We were all a story to her. Everything was a story to her. Liddy was just really happy she didn't have to go to a concert.

"You see," Henry said, "the goddess Artemis was really mad because some Greek guy had killed one of her favorite rabbits. So she made sure the winds didn't blow their ships to Troy. Agamemnon conned his daughter, Iphigenia, to come and marry Achilles, who had a vulnerable heel. She was sacrificed. Agamemnon killed his own daughter. Later, the Greeks came to the conclusion they shouldn't kill their kids. They changed the story, and Artemis whisked her away. A fawn was killed instead. I like gods who tell us not to sacrifice our kids when powerful people goof up."

"Perhaps generals everywhere should convert to Greek mythology," I suggested. Elvis nodded in agreement. I glanced at the space where his arm should have been, and I wondered how many other arms were gone. How many legs were missing? My country did this.

My God! My country did this!

I felt the urge to convert to Greek mythology. At that moment, Henry's religion sounded pretty good. Change the story when it involves human sacrifice. Object to the plot when kids are maimed. Break the law when the law becomes arrogant. Rebellion? Revolution? I looked at my own arm and was thankful it existed. That was some sort of answer—my vote in the ballot box.

I wished Noah and Eloise still existed. I wished Elvis still had his arm. Nothing, indeed, is certain, but this was not our moment for blind obedience. I simply vowed to never kneel down to pray to anything or anybody. No. This was our night to defy the system. If windows needed to be broken, we would break them. If doors needed to be knocked down, we would knock them down. If trespass were necessary, we would trespass. If theft were the means to our night's end, deem us good thieves all. I had my answer. The night was very dense. Every sound echoed in the evening air. I heard the bark of every dog.

We weren't exactly Robin Hood and his Merry Men. Liddy hummed the melody to some Bob Dylan tune while Uncle Ho and Elvis conversed with each other. Chiseled in my memory are the stoic lines of their faces, like the images on Mount Rushmore, or some president's picture on a coin. They knew more about America than I did; while I had given up in a chuckle of indifferent sarcasm, they knew that America, in its best attire, is nothing more than an opportunity, a slim heartbeat of a chance to be a bit more educated, a bit more opinionated—a bit more defiant. It offers a chance to have a good job and be better off than so many others in the hungry world. America would allow them to buy shoes for their kids, even if it meant shopping at a discount store. Shoes were shoes.

They knew America had given them each a garden rake, and they knew it was now their opportunity, possibly even their duty, to tend the plants still growing in our fertile American soil. They knew all of this, and I will always respect them for having that wisdom. In time, they, too, would hopefully hum a Bob Dylan tune, just like Liddy Maenad, the woman with flowing blond dreadlocks who sat next to me as we drove off to rescue Dara from some hellhole of a puppy mill smack-dab in the middle of my America.

Jenny Ego drove her red Ford Zephyr. Of course, she sped. Jenny was not one to be confined by the restraints of reality.

I followed.

She drove faster; I couldn't keep up with her. If she were, indeed, writing this bit of the story, then she was in the midst of a sudden burst of inspiration, and the words, with both defiance and deliberation, were exceeding the speed limit—as well she should.

But I was the one who was caught! For a hopeful moment, I thought the flashing lights would speed past me. Perhaps it was somebody else's turn to be guilty. Damn! Wrong place and wrong time. Someone had to pay. I knew it! I glanced into my mirror, but that really wasn't necessary. The police lights circulated through the interior of the car. Uncle Ho's face was suddenly red; then he was blue; then he was the bright white of a street lamp. The same was true for Liddy. In an odd way, the whole thing resembled a psychedelic light show some hippy rock band used for groovy effects while playing its West Coast revolutionary music from the sixties counterculture.

HE DIDN'T THINK SO — TWICE!

It was the wrong time to be sarcastic. I knew it then, and I know it today. But the opportunity was too much.

I looked into the policeman's face. Damn, again. It was Colonel Mustard! Well, that wasn't his real name.

We all knew Mean Mister Mustard. He was Officer Clue — like the guy from a murder-mystery board game. Officer Morrison Clue — like Morrison Hotel, but this guy's temperament didn't exude Holiday Inn hospitality. He was a bully who unfortunately saw law enforcement as a means to perpetuate his obvious lack of humanity. He was just a nasty person who managed to get a badge. So we called him Colonel Mustard from the Clue board game. Sometimes, it was changed to Mean Mr. Mustard, like the song by the Beatles.

It's a shame because there's always one in every crowd. There are so many others who are decent people, but there is always one, one Mean Mr. Colonel Mustard. Every town, it seems, has its cruel joke, and he was our local punch line. I knew what to expect. I looked at Officer Clue with the red, blue, and bright flashlight shining in my eyes. I was simply fed up with the routine and its daily footsteps upon the walkways that never bothered to be anything other than concrete. It suddenly occurred to me to say, "Look, I'm really in a hurry. So, whatever you are selling, I'm just not interested."

Well, that certainly was the wrong thing to say! Really, how was I to explain that we were following behind a Ford Zephyr driven by the possible author of the story in which we all existed, and we were going to save her dog, Dara, and hopefully Dara's puppy who would allow us to save oak trees who had names like Erna, Thecla, Peter, Paul, and Moses? Should I have told him about the tuberculosis, and the war stories, and Mrs. Fletcher's music lessons, and Roswell Robbie's semiautomatic gun, and the silver alien space suits, and Belle's legs that no longer worked very well?

Should I have told him about old Otis, who always needed a haircut? How could I explain the excitement that old dog exuded as he chased a ball when I mentioned Pete Rose and Babe Ruth? Should I have mentioned Thomas Goast and Franklin, and Noah and Eloise, who were no longer Noah and Eloise, and should I have mentioned the naked Digger guy with the long beard and wire-rimmed glasses who took a picture of some words etched into the heartwood of a tree that somehow helped our Green Bay Packers beat the Chicago Bears?

What about Henry Thumm, a practicing Greek Mythologist who was arrested because they thought he was a Druid? How could I explain Uncle Ho, the old Vietnamese grandfather whose name wasn't even Uncle Ho? Or Elvis, whose name really was Elvis. Who would believe all of that? No one. So I just said, "So, whatever you're selling, I don't want any." In a weird way, I suppose, it was my way of politely saying, "Don't tread on me tonight." Because that's the way I felt and, as you know, I was never one to get angry.

Apparently, Colonel Mustard didn't see it my way at all. He didn't have much of a sense of humor, like God in Adam's version of Genesis. Neither the flashlight nor his gruff voice laughed at my attempt at humor. "I know you." That's what he said. "You're that guy who wrote that drug song!"

"No," I said, "it wasn't about drugs, officer, honest. It was about oleomargarine."

"Oleomargarine?" he asked.

Then we both heard Liddy's voice from within the car say, "You know— oleomargarine. It's a well-known butter substitute." It was such a great thing to say. I was in love with this woman!

HE DIDN'T THINK SO — TWICE!

Then Officer Clue made her get out of the car, too. The cop flashed his light at her. She was still wearing the high heels, nylons, and her sexy white dress. "What's a nice-looking girl like you doing with a guy like this?"

I had to agree. The officer had a valid point. Sure, he was a bully, but he still had a valid point. But I didn't nod in agreement. I was frozen in the fear of what I knew would be Liddy's certain reaction. My life flashed before me, and I remembered every kick and every punch. I don't know very much, but I know that assault and battery on a police officer beats a speeding ticket every time. I just closed my eyes because this was not going to be a pretty sight.

Well, Heaven be praised! Perhaps it was the confines of her sexy dress. Perhaps it was the awkwardness of those heels. Perhaps it was the compliment, or maybe she was relieved because she didn't have to go to the REO Speedwagon and Styx concert with that pet shop boy. Perhaps it was the sight of a second police car arriving. Who knows? I am eternally grateful because Lydia stowed her anger long enough for us to recognize the second officer as none other than Tim Paine, the police officer who later would be murdered during a routine midnight patrol as he stopped someone who decided to act like a shotgun, rather than a human being.

After all these years, knowing the fate of Officer Tim Paine — a genuinely great person — and remembering him as he conversed with Colonel Mustard, I simply have to add to my list of questions to ask God. You know, ice cream and Italy are great things, but why do decent people have to die so young? Why do nasty people live to a silly old age — an age that allows them to be silly old nasty people? Perhaps there was nothing that could ever be done with Canada.

THE GOSPEL ACCORDING TO DARA

Officer Paine knew me and smiled. Then he saw Uncle Ho and Elvis in the backseat of the car. I knew exactly what Uncle Ho was thinking. Liddy did, too. We all realized Uncle Ho was a man who understood our law did not always protect everyone. It had not protected his grandson. America is a beautiful idea, but America, sometimes, is simply an experiment—or a gold mine—that doesn't quite pan out.

Thomas Edison, in his attempt to illuminate the darkness, tried six thousand bits of vegetable matter in his light bulb. He tried cedar thread fiber. That didn't work. Mark Twain wrote *The Adventures of Huckleberry Finn* and his "The War Prayer." Edison tried boxwood. Eugene Debbs was sentenced to ten years in jail for saying he wasn't any better than anybody else on the face of the planet. Rosa Parks waited hundreds of years to be unfettered from the filthy bowels of a slave ship and finally sat where she so desired in the front of a city bus. She was arrested. Edison tried hickory. He failed—just like the student protest march at Kent State University in 1970 where kids were shot and killed by the National Guard who were sworn to protect their rights. Edison tried bamboo. We napalmed Vietnam and brought them democracy. George Bush attacked Iraq. Edison tried baywood. George W. Bush attacked Iraq again. Edison tried flax.

That's the American way—try everything at the buffet bar.

Thomas Edison eventually struck incandescent gold with carbonized cotton thread filament. He illuminated houses, businesses, libraries, and schools. The corner streetlight under which we talked with Officer Mustard Clue was lighted with brutal clarity. I looked at Uncle Ho, the old man who had lost his grandson to uncertain justice and sadly realized the filament has yet to be found to ignite all the words in the libraries, schools, and perhaps the local coffee shop—a filament—an alchemist stone—with enough magic to transform the lead of what we Americans are into the gold of what we have always promised to be.

Officer Paine settled things, for once, his own way. "I'll take care of this," he said to Colonel Mustard. The officer looked hesitant, even angry; but this was Tim Paine's call. There was never any question about it. When Officer Clue drove away, Tim Paine spoke to Uncle Ho and Elvis. Then he turned to Liddy and me and simply said, "Just follow behind me. We'll take care of this whole thing."

So history repeated itself. Thank goodness for that. I remembered my Polish grandfather, and I envisioned him as he walked behind the police horse hoping his children would have a better life, a life where they wouldn't be killed just for being at the wrong place at the wrong time, a life where a dad could afford to buy his kid a pair of new shoes. Sometimes, America can be a place like that. Uncle Ho and Elvis, like my grandfather, had found their police officer who was decent enough to offer a helping hand—a light in the strange darkness of an American night.

Jenny Ego was already at the house.

We followed Officer Paine into the narrow driveway. His lights flashed and illuminated a sign that warned: BEWARE OF DOG! There were no lights in the house, but the streetlight cast a dim glow on the old porch. There were mice everywhere, and there were too few traps. No one had even bothered to remove the mouse carcasses, which were, for the most part, just tiny skeletons with huge teeth still gripping molding pieces of cheese. I wondered if these mice would have preferred oleomargarine. There were ants all around the traps and the dead mice.

We could hear the dogs whining inside.

"Don't we need a search warrant?" I asked.

Officer Paine didn't say a word.

The dogs just kept whining.

Jenny Ego tried the door. It was locked. "I know my Dara is in there!" she screamed. She punched at the door. Henry Thumm cupped his hands and tried to see through the window. Officer Paine pushed against the door, which refused to open. He stood for a second to gather strength for another attempt when, suddenly, a strange halo of light illuminated his body. It was a searchlight. Another police car arrived. I heard several doors slam in no particular order, and there were several more searchlights, all focused on that front door.

The chief of police was there. His name was Buddy King, but everyone called him King Bud because he was so arrogant. The guy thought he ruled the city with some sort of divine right. He had one of those bullhorns to amplify his every word. That was odd because he was only ten feet from us as we stood on the mouse-infested porch. In the shadow of the police chief—with only a vague silhouette to suggest his presence—stood Thomas Goast.

We all knew who did the talking. "Now, Tim," King Bud said slowly, "we're just here to help out. You know that." Officer Paine held his ground. "Now, remember, Tim," King Bud warned. "Remember who's in charge." Officer Paine refused to move. "Let's just make this an order," King Bud said.

"What kind of order?" Lydia shouted. "Two cheeseburgers with everything?" That was a truly brilliant carhop American thing to say!

"No," King Bud said. "I want Officer Paine here to get back in his car and drive away. This situation is under control." Then he walked forward, still holding that silly megaphone— no different from the microscope of Mo Rainbow's grade-school warning. They both simply magnified our arrogance. He stepped right through the remains of all those dead mice. The megaphone must have been on because the entire universe heard the sound of those mouse skeletons crackling and popping under the weight of his police shoes, like Jiffy-pop kernels bouncing around in hot tin foil. The pop heard 'round the world. Even in the darkness, I could see all the ants running for cover. I didn't blame them. King Bud walked right up to Officer Paine. "I told you to get in your car and leave," he said.

"I would," Tim Paine said, "but someone's got to give a damn about the poor dogs in there. You know. Somebody's just got to give a damn."

King Bud looked at Henry Thumm. "Don't I know you? Weren't you one of those Druid people we arrested?"

Henry didn't say a word. He just stood there. Poseidon would have been proud of him.

He looked at me. "Aren't you that drug kid? I thought you died of a heroin overdose? Why aren't you dead? You should be dead."

"Sorry to disappoint," I said.

The guy actually looked sad. Then he looked at Liddy who stood next to me. "What's a good-looking girl like you doing hanging around with him?"

He had a valid point.

The dogs whined. They had a valid point, too.

King Bud glanced at Uncle Ho and Elvis and told them, "You know this place can't cash your welfare checks, so why don't you just go home?" He turned to Tim Paine and told him again to get in his car and drive away. Officer Paine did not leave. "By God," our chief of police said, "Paine! You will do graveyard shift until, by God I swear, Frosty the snowman begs for a fur coat because it's so damn cold in Hell!"

THE GOSPEL ACCORDING TO DARA

That was, of course, a death sentence, but we didn't know it at the time. I clearly remember it all. Officer Paine stood there, forever burning, like the best of all filaments, into the gun sight retinas of King Bud's eyes. I remember the sound of those mice skeletons as they crackled and popped in the magnified electricity of the moment.

"I don't think so." That's exactly what Tim Paine said to King Bud. The guy just gave a damn. He said he didn't think so, with the searchlight in his eyes. That's what we told King George in our revolution. We just said that we didn't think so—we gave a damn. Judas was not needed to deliver the fateful kiss. Officer Timothy Paine was caught in the searchlight, like a prisoner of war on a barbed-wire fence clinging to what he deemed to be his duty.

I saw a thousand thankless midnight patrols, with his wife at home; a thousand midnight patrols with the people of the night, and the night fears, and the night dangers. I saw his kids at home, who just understood enough to know their dad worked nights and couldn't watch their favorite shows on TV. Then I watched as this great man, Officer Paine, walked slowly to his police car and came back cradling this big heavy tube designed to break down doors. He hit the door with a heavy thud. That would be a great name for a rock band—A Heavy Thud—because the door caved into itself. The doors always cave into themselves. Play the right rock song. Blow the wigs off the rich people. Officer Paine hit the door again, and that was it. In a moment, we found all the dogs. They were whining and barking in every stuffed corner of the place. One cage door was opened. Then more were opened, and there were Irish setters everywhere. There were dachshunds and shelties all over the place—all caged for the convenience of puppy profiteers.

HE DIDN'T THINK SO—TWICE!

Jenny yelled, "Dara! Where are you, Dara?"

Hundreds of dogs just barked and whined.

The only light was from a dim bulb suspended from the ceiling. They hadn't even bothered with a shade. But that dim bulb revealed everything. If anybody has ever wondered where our society stashed all the empty beer cans, cigarette butts, and crumpled potato-chip bags, well, this was the place. This was the answer.

A guy named Jimmy Zen, who was in a punk band called Bored Money, once told me aliens from outer space posed no threat to humanity. He said they would become addicted to alcohol, cigarettes, and junk food, just like the rest of us here on Earth. He didn't even bother to mention our fondness for casino gambling. Henry Thumm, I recall, once nodded in quick agreement when I said space aliens came here for Cedar Crest ice cream. Quite frankly, I prefer my space aliens to be lactose tolerant.

The humans, using the term loosely, had trashed the place. Apparently, the people who ran this place drank beer, smoked too many cigarettes, and loved potato chips. I saw several pit bulls in really small cages, and I felt bad for them.

Jenny continued to yell, "Dara! Where are you, Dara?"

We all heard the bark. I know dogs are possessions and are just property to our legal system, but I swear I heard a sublime voice. Sure, it was a setter's bark, but it was a voice. It was a voice asking for compassion and begging for wisdom. It was only the bark of a dog, but what a wonderful sound it was to hear. Then Jenny saw her Dara. The entire universe saw her Dara, who danced on the awful steel bars of her cage. She knew her human.

Some people believe that dancing is a gift from God. Well, if that is true, then Dara's dance was a prayer, a lovely thing to see. It resembled the motion captured in a Degas ballerina painting. No. Quite frankly, it was much more beautiful than any Degas painting.

Jenny put her hand against the bars of Dara's cage, and Dara stretched her long setter body against the small confines of her cage. Her paws pushed forward and squeezed their way beneath the metal of the door. Those paws reached to touch Jenny's palm. It was a sight to see.

But that wasn't enough. We had to find Dara and old Otis' puppy. That puppy would ensure Erna and all the other old oak trees could live. Through the light of that dim bulb, I surveyed the room. I laughed. It was, I suppose, a final sarcastic moment.

King Bud cursed out loud as he stood behind me.

I laughed again.

Then every eyeball looked into the dusty corner where the cobwebs were spun with caution and sympathy. This was the place of no return—with dogs of no certain breed. This was a no-man's land for dogs. No one really wanted these dogs. No one really wanted this place because there was no profit in this place. Here was a sign that clearly read: THESE DOGS ARE UNFIT FOR MALL SALE! DISPOSE OF THEM!

I looked at one dog. He was tiny, and he had only one eye. I understood all about this place. This was the death camp. Here were the misfits, the half-breeds, the dogs with imperfections and abnormalities, hidden, and not for sale in our perfect society. They were the undesired byproducts of a machine.

Sure, these dogs in the forgotten corner were all mutts. They were the offspring of uncertain origin—no use to any mall pet store. They didn't fit with the perfect fountain and perfect dance classes. These were the dogs nobody wanted. They were the hungry, the tired, and the neglected. They were destined for the landfill.

HE DIDN'T THINK SO—TWICE!

In my mind, these dogs will always be like a black-and-white photo in a history textbook. Huddled together, they reminded me of an immigrant family as they stared at the camera. This family was scared, with no place else to go. I had always known a warm home. I always had a place to go. So I could not understand their eyes. They had heard about this thing called electricity. They knew candles. But they wanted this greater light. That's what I wanted—a greater light. That's what Thomas Edison—a truly great American—wanted to see.

Then I saw one puppy with little stubby little legs and a certain setter look. The little dog barked right at me. I saw that little dog. He had a goatsbeard patch of hippy two-fingered, peace-loving hair standing erect and defiant on the very top of his puppy head. No comb could ever control those hairs—outlaws as they were—of the follicle world. This was a bad case of terminal cowlick. He barked, and the sound was absolutely lovely, like a Polish folk melody, the kind my grandfather once played.

This was the puppy that could save the trees.

"So what?" I heard Thomas Goast's voice. "This doesn't make any difference. Those trees are still coming down. It's just a matter of time." I saw a grim grin.

The puppy barked again, making a high-pitched playful sound—like any puppy bark into the staid world of obedience training—and I knew what he meant. He was happy, and he was just telling the world that he didn't think so, either.

the Gospel of Joshua Toss

EVERYONE WITH WHOM I SPOKE suddenly seemed really happy, but they weren't happy about Dara and her puppy. Quite frankly, I don't really think anyone knew or cared about the trees and the dogs.

"Did you watch the debate?" someone in the grocery checkout line said to the cashier.

"No," she answered. "I work here all the time. I don't get to watch much television."

"I saw it," someone else said. "Carter didn't even bother to show."

"He's probably praying those Arabs release the hostages."

Somebody laughed.

I stood in a long grocery store line with all sorts of puppy supplies in my shopping cart. Apparently, Ronald Reagan, the man who would soon be president, had scored a big victory with the voting public when he said something about America being "a shining city on some hill." Everybody seemed really upbeat about his words. We in America like to think of ourselves as morally superior to the rest of the word. The pilgrims started all that stuff. They didn't like witches or anyone else who disagreed with their views, so we still mention God on our coins. Other countries don't seem to have this concern.

We Americans like it when our politicians say things about being some beacon for the rest of the world; and when they say those words, we usually elect them to public office because they perpetuate the myth of America as the shining city on an important hill. This sort of comment makes us feel really great, and we Americans like to feel great as we go about our affluent American lives, which God prefers over some country whose name I still can't pronounce, a country that makes our T-shirts to be sold in our fancy air-conditioned malls.

Nobody liked Jimmy Carter.

He told us all in a television interview that Americans shouldn't be so greedy, and while wearing a thick cardigan sweater, he told us to conserve energy because we used too much of it. Unfortunately, Jimmy Carter couldn't free the Americans the Iranians took as hostages. We didn't like that at all. People who live in the shining city on the hill never do anything to justify being taken hostage.

I think it all had something to do with oil and the deposed Shah of Iran and his need for cancer treatment.

Believe me—I was just trying to buy a few necessities for our new puppy while standing in the grocery store checkout line. The store's manager had a friend who had a friend who had a cousin who was related to one of the hostages. So he was really happy with Ronald Reagan's surge in popularity. There were flags all over the store. It was just like the Fourth of July, except it was the middle of September. The manager was caught up in the euphoria of the Reagan Revolution. He offered a great deal on eggs because it was "morning in America again, and every morning in America people always need eggs." The bacon was the same price it had always been. Believe me—I just wanted to buy a few puppy supplies. That's all I wanted to do.

"Yeah," someone said, "Reagan will nuke those Iranians."

I read the tabloid headlines of the magazines proclaiming someone had lost weight, a fish could compute complex mathematical problems, and the Fountain of Youth had, at last, been found somewhere in Florida.

"Reagan will nuke the Commies," someone said. "He hates the Commies."

"Moscow will glow at night," someone else said. Everybody in the checkout line laughed. I wanted to feel patriotic, but I wasn't certain I wanted Moscow to glow at night. I wasn't planning to vote for Reagan, but I still wanted to feel patriotic. I just couldn't laugh about nuclear bombs.

Uncle Sam suddenly appeared. Well, it wasn't really Uncle Sam. It was Dan Ott, a local kid who never quite graduated from high school but worked as a hired hand at several of the local farms. He was a big kid and a former high school wrestler who always wore bib overalls while he restocked the dairy shelves in the grocery stores. We called him Dairy Dan because he smelled like cheese curds. Dan was dressed as Uncle Sam. Apparently, a second cousin of George Bush, Sr., the future vice president and president, was coming to the area to court the dairy farmers' vote. This was a big deal. That's why Dairy Dan wore the Uncle Sam getup. Dan looked just like Uncle Sam as he gave the customers cheese curds and American flags. The cheese curds had been dyed red, white, and blue. He saw me and became agitated—in a Joseph McCarthy sort of way. "You're that guy," he said. "You're that guy who wrote that song."

Believe me—I was just in the grocery store buying some pet toys for the new puppy.

THE GOSPEL OF JOSHUA TOSS

"I know," I confessed. I gave into the inevitable, thinking about the long and winding road of questions and accusations. "Sure, it was a drug song. It was a drug song. You figured it out. Congratulations, you're Uncle Sam, and you've won a prize. For all I care, you can win a war." I was just fed up with telling the truth. "If you want it to be a drug song," I offered, "then take it. It's your drug song. It's 'Lucy in the Sky with Oleomargarine.'"

"A drug song?" Dairy Dan said.

"Yeah," I said. "You figured it out." I truly didn't care anymore.

"That wasn't a drug song," he said.

"It wasn't?"

"No," he said, "it was about smuggling oleomargarine into our dairy state."

"It was?"

"Sure."

"Are you really sure?" I asked in disbelief. Here was a brother in arms, and I wanted to hug the guy. Instead, I took a red cheese curd and proudly ate it. We were brothers in arms! I ate another red cheese curd. We were brothers in cholesterol accumulation!

"Sure," Dairy Dan explained. Then he pointed his Uncle Sam finger right between my eyes. He looked exactly like the war poster I had seen a thousand times. "And it still pisses me off!" he screamed.

I no longer wanted to hug the guy.

Uncle Sam yelled at me, and it wasn't a Lydia yell. He sounded like one of those drill sergeants in a boot camp from hell. Let's see, I was a communist, un-American, a vegetarian, and probably a Chicago Bear fan. He even accused me of being intolerant of lactose-tolerant people.

I tried to laugh and said I preferred my space aliens to have a sweet tooth for ice cream.

THE GOSPEL ACCORDING TO DARA

But he kept shouting, as a number of fellow shoppers began to gather to watch Uncle Sam persecute a heathen, a cow-hater, a criminal who advocated the use of oleomargarine, that well-known butter substitute. Some woman reading a tabloid article titled "Pet Cat Learns Sign Language from Deaf Toddler" told the mob she had seen me once in a restaurant eating a piece of apple pie without the requisite slice of cheese.

There was a gasp of disbelief!

Uncle Sam took one of the tiny American flags he had been giving away as a cheese-curd promotion, raised the flag like it was a crucifix, and acted like he was performing an exorcism. He waved that tiny flag right in front of my eyes. It was so close I could read the small sticker. That small sticker simply read, "Made in China."

Ouch!

The Sirens of sarcasm called my name. An American flag shouldn't be made in China. This was wrong! Let the Chinese people make their own damn flag! It's just an idea, but we have laws and rules for so many things. We have laws about sidewalks in our neighborhoods, automobile exhaust emissions, and begging on street corners. We even had a law that prohibited the use of oleomargarine — a well-known butter substitute — in the state of Wisconsin. Perhaps we should have a regulation that makes sure any semblance of our American flag is made in America by an American worker — earning a living wage — a person who has some awareness of the real price paid for those stars and stripes, a price that is never figured into a monthly MasterCard statement.

I just got fed up. Sometimes that happens. I felt like I had eaten one too many plates of everything offered at the local Chinese buffet. That stuff tastes so good at first, but then it cons the taste buds into thinking one more eggroll will somehow alleviate an American desire for satisfaction. That's all we really want—satisfaction—but America is about the possibility of more of everything—the unlimited buffet—the great return on our investment—so we are always hungry, even when our collective stomach says the gas tank is full. I wanted to weep. I had digested too much, and the stuff stuck in my guts wasn't digestible anymore. I tried to spit some sarcastic comment, but the words evaporated before I could say them. I was over-whelmed with humanity's empty beer cans, cold cigarette butts, discarded potato-chip wrappers, arrogance, and tabloid truth. Wisdom was met with disinterest, and compassion was buried in an unmarked grave. Moses was dead, and nobody did any-thing about it. Belle couldn't walk, so they gave her a wheelchair. Some Chinese guy made American flags, which were just some-thing for sale, like the puppy supplies I wanted to buy. Noah and Eloise were for sale. Elvis was for sale. Every breath I took was for sale. And for crying out loud, Dairy Dan, who smelled like a giant cheese curd and looked like Uncle Sam, was still yelling in my face about democracy and dairy products.

I echoed the words Walter Cronkite said when he under-stood the truth about Vietnam. I repeated his words. I had noth-ing better to say, and I had no better way to say what I felt while Uncle Sam was lecturing me about the evils of oleomargarine and breaking the law.

So I yelled, "What the hell is going on?" The woman in front of me didn't know what to think. She was fairly young, very tan, and I didn't know she was wearing a blond wig until she fell backward and the darn thing flew off her head. Her own hair was short, brown, and curly. The fancy blond wig just made her look expensive—like something else for sale. Truly, she was no different from the sugary donuts for sale next to fancy decorated birthday cakes—which were marked as "yesterday's bakery."

I felt bad, but I couldn't stop screaming about the Chinese people making our American flags. It really mattered to me. I just thought Americans should make our flag, and the Chinese should make their flag. I kept screaming all of this while imagining Moses bleeding from the bullet holes in his head and chest. I saw Belle without any legs. I held old Otis again. I cried and screamed until I was bone dry. I didn't have a sarcastic thing to say. I just decided to walk away from the buffet. I couldn't laugh. That's why I screamed. "What the hell is going on?" I yelled again.

The tan woman tried to put on her blond wig.

I really didn't care.

Somebody called security.

I kept yelling. Quite frankly, everything I was screaming made perfect sense to me. Moses. Otis. Belle. Noah and Eloise. American flags made by some Chinese person. It all made perfect sense. I knew how wonderful America was when it just lets itself listen to its rivers, mountains, and cornfields. Hitch a ride with a car full of girls with cut off jeans. Stand on the shore of Lake Michigan at midnight and understand the beauty—a beauty without a price tag. Sure, I always knew about the awful stuff, but I started to scream because the bad stuff was suddenly everywhere, and there just wasn't enough beauty anymore for me to muster the strength to don the jester's garb and defuse the dynamite by telling a joke.

To everyone else, however, it was just gibberish, a voice from the wilderness of old oak trees shouting at the architects and tenants of high-rise Babylon. So they called security again—but this was a grocery store. There was no security. They had cereal, canned fruit, Coke and Pepsi products, fresh seafood, silly get-well cards, and frozen pizzas, but they didn't have any security. That's why I was grabbed and manacled by an Uncle Sam look-alike, who pointed a finger at me and said, "I want you!"

Dan Ott had been a varsity high school wrestler. He had me down on the floor with a quick wrestling move I should have expected, except for the fact that I never paid attention in gym class. I kept screaming about Chinese people making our flags. Uncle Sam wanted me to shut up. I didn't want to shut up, so I was wrestled to the ground.

The floor of the grocery store smelled like fruit, and Dairy Dan smelled like an oversized cheese curd. I was taken down because other people needed to shop, and I was in their way. America is, after all, about shopping. They never stopped the music that made the shopping experience a bit more pleas-ant. While my head was flat against the cold tiles that smelled like fruit, the song "Fortunate Son" by Creedence Clearwater Revival played in the soft distance of the store's hidden speak-ers. I will always remember that song because I was face down on the grocery store floor when I heard it playing. That's not easily forgotten.

I wasn't arrested. They took me to place where they needed to take my belt. I told them it wasn't necessary. The on-duty psy-chiatrist's name was, believe it or not, Dr. Snow. I remembered Dr. Rein. I smiled and said, "If you have a shrink friend named Dr. Sleet, I need to talk to him. Then the post office people will have to make me an honorary mailman."

He didn't respond to my comment. He just looked at his notes. "It says here that you have a problem with anger."

"Well, that's one way of looking at it," I told him.

He asked me if I was all right.

THE GOSPEL ACCORDING TO DARA

I thought for a bit longer than he cared to listen and finally said I thought I was all right.

He nodded.

I asked if Liddy had come to see me. That was an important thing to say. But she couldn't see me. I wondered if she still wore that white dress, and I felt terribly alone until someone directed me to a room to talk with the other people who had problems with anger. There were no clocks, so I had no idea of the passage of time. I didn't mind. Seconds passed. Minutes passed. I didn't mind. Hours. Days. I didn't know, but I didn't mind. I may have been in that place for twenty years. They had a few magazines in the room, for which I was quite grateful. They were those magazines usually found in a dentist's office when I was a kid. One had a puzzle page that asked, "What's Wrong with This Picture?"

The cartoon, which was a depiction of a fancy resort hotel, had several things that didn't fit in the picture. The object was to find the wrong stuff. This can really keep a person busy. I found more than the magazine people had intended for me to find. I really wanted to find a picture of some Chinese person making an American flag, but I couldn't find one. Perhaps it was there, and I just couldn't see it. In the future, someone can look for weapons of mass destruction. They won't be there either. Sometimes, that happens. Perhaps they will be in a different issue of the magazine.

I sat next to a woman who calmly told me she was a very violent person. Her name tag said *Theresa*. The woman who was in charge was friendly and told me this was a group-therapy session. I had no choice, unlike later, when I would choose the car with the teenaged girls with their feet sticking out of the windows instead of the car with the elderly couple with the great big sunglasses. The woman held a brown paper bag and said we all had to write a message to the person next to us. I looked at Theresa. She confessed and told me she was a violent person. What did I have to say to her? She was very polite. That was strange, considering her stark admission. Perhaps this was a real life "what's wrong with this picture?" and she was the weird item to be found and circled.

"Why are you here?" I asked.

"I told you," she said. "I'm a violent person."

"Are you really violent?" I asked.

"Yes, I am." She said this while looking at me with the kindest eyes I have ever seen. She paused patiently and said in a quiet voice, "I'm only violent to myself."

"What do you mean?" I glanced quickly at her wrists. There were no cut marks. "Did you try to kill yourself?" I asked.

"I would never do that."

"No?"

"I would never do that because then I couldn't be violent anymore. And I enjoy being violent."

"But only to yourself?"

"Only to myself." I glanced again at her wrists. I thought about Elvis and that missing part of his arm. "Oh," she said slowly, "don't look there. I don't slice myself there." She tapped the center of her chest. One finger touched her name tag. "I cut myself here," she said.

"Your heart?"

"No," she smiled. "What's the heart? I want this wound to fester forever. So I carve into my soul."

I decided she was a spooky violent person.

"I do it for love," she confessed.

"Love?"

"Yes," she said. "Jesus suffered for love. My husband says I should suffer for his love. He's a Christian. So he's right."

"Why don't you leave him?"

"Nobody can ever leave Jesus," she said.

"No. Your husband. Why don't you leave him?"

"That's what my friends tell me to do."

"So why don't you leave him, then?"

"She looked a bit confused. "I already told you that. I am an extremely violent person."

"But only to yourself." I repeated her words.

She continued to smile. "That's right. Now you understand why I could never leave the man I love."

I could only nod in response. Over the years, I have developed a habit of nodding whenever I order a beer. That's because I wanted a beer after listening to Theresa, the woman who had such kind eyes. I still remember Theresa's confession and her eyes. That's probably why I nod whenever I order a drink.

"So what did they get you for?" Theresa asked.

"Well," I said. "I was mad because they shot this Vietnamese guy and nobody cared."

"Did they shoot him in Vietnam or America?" she asked.

"Does it really make a difference?"

That's what I said.

That's what I asked.

She thought about it for a moment. "I suppose not."

Those were important words.

So I said, "And Otis died, and they cut down two beautiful old oak trees."

She agreed with me again. "I'd be mad, too."

"I found out our American flags are made in China."

"That bothered you?"

"Yeah. Then Uncle Sam nabbed me and wrestled me to the ground."

"Well," she said, "that would bother me. That would bother me a lot." She paused. "You see, I can't eat dairy because I'm a vegan. I don't believe in harming animals." She was so incredibly kind, and yet she was so incredibly violent. "My husband hunts, and he calls me a fool."

"About being a vegetarian?"

"No," she said. "He just calls me a fool about everything I do." She paused. "Hey!" she said to a man in a wheelchair. The guy wore an army fatigue jacket. "This guy is in here because he was angry about China making American flags. What do you think?"

The guy in the wheelchair had a Vietnam stare. He never said a word.

When the brown paper bag came to me, I read the note from the person on my left. Her name tag said "Chilly," and her note to me said, "You seem too nice to be here." I smiled because that was the game we were playing at this therapy session. It was just another restaurant game where we all laughed at jokes that weren't funny. It was yet another lie.

I was uncertain what to write for Theresa. What's there to say to a person who knew she could never leave Jesus or her husband and wanted her soul to bleed for eternity? The Hallmark card people never had to tackle a tough situation like that.

I took too much time.

Everyone watched me.

Then, because I truly could not think of anything else to say, I wrote, "We've gotta get out of this place, if it's the last thing we ever do." I always liked this song lyric by the Animals. It just made some sort of sense to write this on the blank piece of paper. It's just a great song.

THE GOSPEL ACCORDING TO DARA

I was really surprised by Theresa's reaction. I had read Chilly's note in silence. Theresa, who could never leave Jesus or her husband, smiled and nudged the guy seated next to her. She handed him my note. I didn't know we could do that. They took my belt, but they didn't give me a rule book. The guy next to her looked familiar. Honest to God — it was Jonathan Maenad, Liddy's brother. He was all cleaned up.

Jonathan was, if you recall, the guy who became a bit of a local legend because he wrote a song called "Serfing USA." Business people in the area got behind his song and started to make money. Then kids listened to the song's lyrics telling them not to buy stuff on credit and sell away their freedom and to become serfs, just like in the days of the feudal system. The kids took this message to heart. Sales at the mall plummeted. The businessmen had to stop this shopping plague, so they did the only thing they could do: They ruined Jonathan by giving him anything his rock-star appetite desired. After a while, the poor guy could barely mumble the words to his own song. He was nothing more than a thin impersonation of his former self. That was the end of our local revolution. Kids started to buy stuff again. They even continued, ironically, to buy copious copies of his "Serfing USA" single.

Jonathan looked like the icon from years before who had sung his protest song. He looked good. He looked like he could remember the words to his song. He wasn't smoking or holding a paper bag with a bottle inside or asking people for the food they had not finished and were about to throw into the restaurant dumpster. He looked right at me. Then he looked at my note, the note I had written to Theresa, the woman with an eternal incision cut into her soul. He simply started to sing the words I had written on that piece of paper. He looked great, and his voice was pure, rich, and beautiful, just like the gold people painted around the heads of martyrs and angels in Bible pictures. He sang that song by the Animals, "We Gotta Get out of This Place." Of course, he knew the words. I would have liked to hear him sing "Serfing USA," but this was just as great. It was probably the same thing.

Several of the patients in the ward began to dance. I watched as they paired up and began to slow dance to the song. A slow dance is an answer to just about everything that is sad in the universe. There were no clocks, so I really didn't know how much time ticked into eternity. Thankfully, the lights were dimmed. Mental-health patients don't like bright lights. Jonathan Maenad continued to sing, and the rest of the people continued their beautiful slow dance.

As I watched, I swear they transformed. Two of the dancers from our ward suddenly became lighter than air. They were quiet dervishes who lip-synched some unknown magical word. The dim lights shone right through them. I felt a fresh gust of wind. Then they were Noah and Eloise. They danced on a beautiful wind. This was all my imagination—an imagination resonating with a tune that shook the walls of Jericho. In that moment, my imagination was more durable than a man with a silly gas-powered chainsaw could ever hope to be. I saw Noah and Eloise dancing. Eloise wore a white dress, nylons, and high heels, just like Liddy. I looked at another couple, and they, too were transformed. I saw Mrs. Fletcher, our Thecla Fetcher, dancing with a man in a German uniform.

This didn't make any sense to me at the time. Some years later, Franklin came to see me. Franklin thanked me for saving the trees. He was truly happy and apparently had put a few ghosts to rest. I believe ghosts like it when we put them to rest. I told him about the night in the mental-health ward when I saw his aunt dancing with a man in a German uniform. Franklin told me his aunt had studied music in Berlin and had fallen in love with a man. As Adolf Hitler became a reality, his aunt left Germany. She never heard from her lover—her wonderful Berlin musician. He was, she assumed, just another casualty of war, as was her heart.

So many others danced with my imagination. Sure, Eloise and Noah were there, and Erna was there, too. She was just a child in a white dress, freed from tubercular nightmares. She danced a white-dress dance while standing on the toes of Paul, the fighter pilot who was killed the day after he posed in a sepia photo filled with sepia smiles.

Paul wore his uniform, but he had no medals because he was killed before he could even shoot down an enemy plane. Moses was there, too. He stood patiently behind an empty wheelchair—gently holding its handles. This was a wheelchair waiting for Belle, a wheelchair waiting for a dance. There is always a wheelchair waiting for a dance.

These ghosts danced because of the music, and they danced because they were family. That was a beautiful thought, and it was a beautiful evening. The imagination can never compete with a microscope; but then again, a microscope can never compete with the imagination. Life is a funhouse venture with so many mirrors and so many metaphors into which we cast a reflection. Life is like any album by the Beatles: Every song is profound, but only one melody can be hummed in any given moment; so a choice is made—a song is sung—and the other tunes softly slip away. I sang along with the final words to Jonathan's song. I whispered, "We gotta get out of this place, if it's the last thing we ever do. There's a better place for me and you." Then I said, "Amen."

One more ghost appeared. I knew her instantly. Debbie Finch was there.

But she wasn't the third-grader with cancer I chanced to notice as I left a church with Liddy. She was my age, with no scar on her forehead, and her hair was long, thick, and black—like a Halloween night. I knew it was Debbie because she wore no disguise at all. She looked through me and said, "You should draw the ghost of a bird."

I said, "Sure."

"You should draw the ghost of me."

I nodded.

"I don't care what you draw," she said, "but please, everybody saw the cancer in my brain, but they didn't see the parts of my brain without cancer. Draw that. Draw a life without cancer."

And I suddenly knew that even the most sincere third-grader—even the most sincere third-grader who could draw birds really well—even that kid could never draw a life without cancer.

So I imagined all the sad pictures I would always leave unfinished.

Debbie suddenly said, "You should marry Liddy." She paused and laughed. It's a comfort to know a ghost can still laugh. Then she said, "And for heaven's sake, you have to be a lot more specific. That song Jonathan sang about a better place for you and me. It needs to be a lot more specific." Her fingers reached silently toward the reality of my world. "Let's face it," she said. "Just about anywhere is better than this place." She laughed a ghost laugh again. That may well have been the only disguise she tolerated.

THE GOSPEL ACCORDING TO DARA

I understood her sarcasm. She beat me at my own game. Damn! Be more specific? A better place? There is no other place. There's simply birth and death—with an eternity between them—an eternity of sad and happy holes into which we, tragically, are too afraid, or just too damn proud, to fall.

Theresa asked me to dance. Jonathan kept singing. I didn't dance with her because her soul would have bled over our lovely oak floor. I declined her offer because I wanted to keep the dance floor spotlessly clean. I could, perhaps, have understood melted drops of authentic dairy land ice cream, but I could not tolerate drops of blood soiling this magical moment because, truly, this was the only home I had that night.

Paradise Left

LIDDY PICKED ME UP THE NEXT DAY. The people at the desk asked if they had taken my belt. I told them it didn't matter. It was raining. What did that mean? She smiled. Her smile was better than any umbrella. I smiled, too. Not a word was spoken until we sat together on the bench underneath the shade of all those oak trees. I held our puppy in my arms. He squirmed a lot, barked, and made countless tiny puppy sounds. The white hairs on his head were much too big for the rest of his body.

Liddy knew about anger, and I did too. The old oaks knew about anger. We both looked at the sunken dirt where old Noah and Eloise had once existed. She asked, "How did it feel?"

"You mean to get mad?"

"Yeah."

I thought about the entire universe for a moment. "I felt the wrong wires touch, and then there was an explosion. Positive and negative don't like each other. Fireworks, like the Fourth of July, you know."

"Uh huh." She moved her feet so the tips of her tennis shoes touched. Then she said, "Are you sure they weren't the right wires finally finding each other?" Perhaps she was correct. Maybe Mrs. Fletcher and Debbie were right, too.

We talked about music and planets spinning in the universe so everything was all right. The immensity of the moment was like a cocoon, and neither of us wanted to leave its embrace. Perhaps we were in love with each other. I can't really say for certain because I really don't know about things like that. Music is music—and love is love. Sometimes they merge, and sometimes not. That's just the way it is with Liddy and me. We are odd bits and pieces of love and music who hold hands and make everything a little more harmonious, a little more humorous, and perhaps a little more receptive to all the starry ideas that have flared for millions of years in the patient glance of the distant evening sky. Perhaps that's what lovers are allowed to do.

I told her my anger was like being right in the middle of some magnificent guitar solo. I was right there as the strings vibrated. I could feel these huge spaces, and I went into those spaces. I wasn't in that grocery store buying pet supplies when I got so mad. That's why they locked me up. They knew that I had somehow escaped.

"Escaped what?"

"The grocery store. The mall. A puppy mill. City Hall. Some sarcastic comment—all of the above."

"Except life. You can't escape life," she suggested. Then she said, *"Born to Run."*

I said, "'Born on the Bayou.'"

She said, "'Born to Be Wild.'"

I just said, "'Wasn't Born to Follow.'"

"You cheated," she said. *"Born* should have been the first word."

"Of course," I said. "I just wasn't born to follow."

We were somehow even, and we were so close together. Our coats brushed, and I knew no raindrop could trickle a pathway between us. I thought about Henry Thumm. He would like the rain and its water because he had that altar to Poseidon in his basement. And Ms. Turnkee: I heard she quit her teaching position because somebody with authority was angry when she had moved Greek mythology into her nonfiction unit. She had taken a job in Troy, a town in northern Wisconsin. Lucky people. Good luck to her.

Franklin couldn't cut the trees because we had the puppy. I suppose Thomas Goast is still waiting in the shadows of his own dreams of power. Moses was dead. I thought about Elvis and Uncle Ho. They, just like my grandfather, had found the policeman who looked after them, at least for a little while. Jenny Ego had her Dara. The very last thing she had said to me was so typical of her. She had told me she was just a character in a story I was writing. So she had thanked me for taking the time to allow her to exist and get her Irish setter back. That was such a kind thing to say.

Then I asked the big question. "Are you…" I said to Liddy. "Are you busy tonight?" That was a big-bang question.

"I have to go to that concert," she said.

"REO Speedwagon and Styx?"

"Yeah." Now I was upset.

She just shrugged. "I want to go," she said.

"Lydia!" I was shocked. I remembered the pet shop guy with his pregnant girlfriend. "I suppose you have to wear that fancy dress and those high heels."

She paused. Quite frankly, it was the most beautiful pause in the universe, because then she said. "I'll wear them if you want me to, but then you'll have to wear a suit and tie. I would prefer to go as we really are. You know. Just you and me." I had a sudden vision of holding her while Styx played "Lady." I knew she was thinking the same thing.

"I won't be able to do that without making some sarcastic comment," I confessed.

"That's why I bought the tickets. I'm not going to change, and you certainly are never going to change. Everybody else, well, I think we're always going to have to get along with people out there who enjoy a double concert bill of REO Speedwagon and Styx. We're stuck with tickets to this life."

I had to agree. Perhaps, and it's just an idea, but too many people want to hear Styx sing "Come Sail Away." But Liddy was right. Nobody can escape life.

Liddy looked at all the beautiful old oak trees. "You know we can't stay here in paradise forever. Someday we'll have to leave," she said.

"Sure," I suggested, "but just because we go to the Styx concert, it doesn't mean we can't come back here. It's not as if we're locked out."

"If no one is in the forest to see the beauty of the trees, are the trees still beautiful?" she asked.

I thought about saying that beauty is timeless, and it exists well beyond our limited perceptions. I could say that sort of thing. I could always say things like that in my sleep. But, instead, I told her, "I'll buy the tickets to the next concert."

"Next concert?"

"Sure," I said. "Captain and Tennille are bound to play in town someday. They're really popular. You can sing along to all their songs."

She gave me that Lydia look.

What can I say? It wasn't exactly the look of love. Rather, it was a look begging to share harmony, humor, and starry ideas that flare in the distant night sky. It was the look that would inspire any Adam to taste a forbidden apple from any forbidden tree.

So I picked up the pup digging in the depressed ground where Noah once stood. I pressed the puppy to my chest and touched those beautiful sprouts of white hair on the top of his head. They looked like a sprig of goatsbeard or, perhaps, two fingers of peace held high by an aging hippy; but most of all, they were the living form of two old trees, two old lovers, Noah and Eloise, who once graced this Earth with enough shade and dignity to allow hands to be held under their leafy glance. Their shade made busy people pause and take a deep drink from the infinite spaces between the seconds of everyday life.

Those hairs came with immense responsibility.

I looked at the puppy and said, "You need a name."

"Otis," Liddy said. "He's an Otis. He's always been an Otis."

Then I knew exactly what to say.

"Otis, I said, "you need a haircut." That's what I said. I told the trees Otis needed a haircut. I told the sky Otis needed a haircut. I told every raindrop Otis needed a haircut. I told the universe. That's what I said, and that's what I hoped to say every spring, forever and ever, when beautiful old oak trees everywhere muster the spirit to blossom and dance slowly in the air, one more time, with the compassion and wisdom found in the warmth of the western wind.

a few More Questions and a few More Answers

So, this is your second book — Do Peter and Molly from The English Setter Dance know Joshua and Lydia?
Well, they are probably in the same phone book — but I seriously doubt if they send Christmas cards. Joshua is very different from Peter, but as I said, they're in the same phone book.

This book has a lot of American references. Is that important?
I'm from Wisconsin, so that's all I know. But we had season tickets to Packer games, and my dad and I sat in the fifty-sixth row — right on the twenty-yard line. From that height I could see much more than the playing field. Yeah — the book goes beyond Lambeau Field. Although, to be quite honest, in Wisconsin — with all the snow — there is always a glare — so it's America through that glare. And don't forget — we drink a lot of beer in Wisconsin. It's America through that beer.

What about "Paradise Left"?
I love the word "left." Try to translate it into other languages. Let's just say that I recently spent some time in Yellowstone National Park. Of course I had to drive home — and it took three days — but that park is still there, and it will be there long after I'm gone. Trees and otters don't need to sell anything.

A FEW MORE QUESTIONS
AND A FEW MORE ANSWERS

Did you ever learn Uncle Ho's real name?
No. His name is just like Elvis's missing arm—which is just like every name on the Vietnam War Wall.

And what about Theresa—you know—the woman who cuts her soul?
She's the absolute beauty of my America. I've talked with her a thousand times. I've driven past her a thousand times. I've ordered coffee from her. I've watched her send her kids to college. She'll bleed for her kids. She'll bleed for the world. She pays taxes and says nice things about teachers. The last time I saw her she was working in a gas station convenience store. I bought some gas, and she had to ask if I wanted glazer sugar donuts.

She had a name tag that read *Theresa*—just like the night I met her in the place where they took my belt and said I was too violent—too violent to care about dogs and trees. I declined her offer of glazer sugar donuts. I waved, and then she waved—like two polite flags who knew they were both made in America.